GUTLESS

GUTLESS

CARL DEUKER

Houghton Mifflin Harcourt
Boston New York

www.hmhco.com

The text was set in Aldus LT STD

The Library of Congress has cataloged the hardcover edition as follows:
Names: Deuker, Carl, author.
Title: Gutless / Carl Deuker.
Description: Boston : Houghton Mifflin Harcourt, 2016. | Summary: "With both good speed and good hands, wide receiver Brock Ripley should be a natural for the varsity team, but he shies from physical contact. When his issues get him cut from varsity, he also loses his friendship with star quarterback Hunter Gates. Now a target for bullying, Brock struggles to overcome his fears and discover that, in his own way, he is brave enough." —Provided by publisher.
Identifiers: LCCN 2015031264
Subjects: | CYAC: Fear—Ficition. | Bullying—Fiction. | Football—Fiction. | Friendship—Fiction. | High schools—Fiction. | Schools—Fiction. | BISAC: JUVENILE FICTION / Sports & Recreation / Football. | JUVENILE FICTION / Social Issues / Bullying. | JUVENILE FICTION / Boys & Men. | JUVENILE FICTION / Social Issues / Friendship.
Classification: LCC PZ7.D493 Gu 2016 | DDC [Fic]—dc23
LC record available at http://lccn.loc.gov/2015031264

ISBN: 978-0-544-64961-3 hardcover
ISBN: 978-1-328-74206-3 paperback

Printed in the United States
DOC 10 9 8 7 6 5 4 3 2 1
4500663071

For Beth, Noah, and Leila

The author wishes to thank Ann Rider,
the editor of this book, for her help.

PART ONE

CHAPTER 1

I don't know what *it* is, but I do know that Hunter Gates had *it*. Not just because he was bigger and stronger than everybody else. He had *it* in the way he cocked his head, the way he looked at you, the way he *didn't* look at you. He let you know that he came first and everyone else followed and that was how it was meant to be. It's why I never liked him, not in middle school, not in high school. And it's also why—until he went full throttle after Richie Fang—I wanted to be his friend.

It was a hot June day when Hunter Gates showed up. I was hanging out with Trevor Marino, Austin Pauley, and the McDermott twins—Rory and Tim. Eighth grade was over; Whitman Middle School was over. You're in between things when you're that age: you can't wait to grow up, but you're scared of it too.

We'd met at the skateboard park by the library at noon and then drifted down to Gilman Park. We had no plans, so we killed time in the shady area between the wading pool and the basketball court, where a half-dozen shirtless high school guys were playing a full-court game.

Every once in a while, one of us would disrespect another guy—say something about his sister's body or his own zits. It was a joke, but there was always the taste of truth to it, so whoever got dissed would chase his tormentor around, pretending to be mad enough to fight. Sometimes the chase would go through the wading pool, which ticked off the mothers hovering over their toddlers. They glared at us, and finally Mrs. Rojas—the woman who'd supervised the wading pool for a million years—told us to leave.

We argued that we hadn't done anything wrong and that America was a free country, but she threw up her thumb like an umpire making a call at home plate. "Out of here. You're too old to be hanging around a wading pool."

Rory McDermott had brought along his soccer ball—we'd all played on the Whitman Wildcats, our middle school's soccer team—so we wandered over to the soccer field and started kicking it back and forth.

Hunter Gates was two years older than us, so he was heading into his junior year. He was bigger, stronger, tougher, and meaner than anybody else.

Every time I saw Hunter, I remembered Jerry Jerzek.

There was nothing special about Jerry. He wasn't smart or funny or athletic. He was just a good guy.

I don't know what Jerry did to Hunter—or if he even did anything. But in seventh grade, right after Halloween, Hunter got on him, and that meant that Hunter's friends got on him too. They said that his ears were too big, that he crapped logs that clogged the school toilets, that his mother'd had sex with an iguana. And then they started calling him Jerry Jumper.

Nobody knew what the joke was. But every time Hunter or one of his buddies—and he had about a dozen in his posse—spotted Jerry, they'd scream, "Jump, Jerry, jump!"

Jerry tried to ignore them, but then they'd come at him and play-slap him on the side of his face until he finally jumped as if he were on an invisible pogo stick. Once Jerry was red in the face and sweating, Hunter would tell him he could stop. "We're just kidding you, Jerry. No hard feelings."

After Hunter and those guys got on him, nobody wanted to be seen with Jerry. It was as if he had diarrhea or something worse. I once saw him throwing up in the bushes before school. Not long after that, he started skipping school, and in February he transferred to McClure on Queen Anne Hill.

* * *

In my fourth grade science class, my teacher once emptied a bottle of iron filings onto a piece of paper and drew a magnet back and forth above them. The filings danced around the paper, drawn to that magnet wherever it went. That's how it was with Hunter Gates. He drew people to him, even if what he was doing made your insides churn.

The reason was simple. Name a sport where a ball bounced, and Hunter was great at it. Not good—great. Football was his best sport. His father started grooming him to be an NFL quarterback from the day he was born. Hunter's Crown Hill junior football team won the league title every year, and then he was great again in middle school. As a high school freshman, he took Crown Hill High from city laughingstock to the brink of the playoffs. Everybody figured he'd just go on being great, but his sophomore year was mediocre. Not bad, but not good—he was just another quarterback. It was the first time he'd been ordinary.

That June day, while I kicked the ball around with the McDermott twins and the other guys, Hunter and his father unpacked their gear and started throwing a football back and forth. His father was a big-shot attorney for an oil company that did fracking in North Dakota, but he didn't ignore Hunter. At every game and most practices, he was on the sidelines—one of those parent volunteers who do nothing but work with their own son.

Whenever I'd seen Hunter's father at a game or practice, he had his arms crossed in front of his chest, a baseball cap pulled down over his eyes, and a grim look on his face. He didn't scream, but he never smiled, either. Tough love is what my dad called it. "His kid has a ton of talent, so he doesn't want him to waste it. Hard to blame him for that."

All of Hunter's passes that late June day were bullets, straight as a string. But no matter how well he threw, his father saw something wrong. His arm wasn't high enough; he was stepping too far forward; his footwork was slow.

I didn't want a father like that, but I did wish my father could go to the park with me, kick a soccer ball around, and just be a dad.

CHAPTER 2

I used to do everything with my dad—basketball, baseball, soccer, hiking, bike riding. He'd been a soccer player at Eastern Washington—sweeper—but he played any sport I wanted to play, except football. My mom made football off-limits because of all the news about concussions. It was no big deal, because in those days I didn't like the game much, especially the tackling part. My dad was good with his hands too, so on rainy days we built bookcases and made wood toys in the basement.

We don't do any of those things anymore.

Now he needs leg braces to help him stand and arm braces to help him keep his balance. It takes two minutes for him to get out of his chair in the living room and walk to the kitchen. He still has his job at the bank, but for a while they were trying to get rid of him. Unless a cure is found, he'll get worse and worse, until one day he won't be able to walk at all. That day might be twenty years away, and it might be five years, but it's coming.

In a way he got sick all at once, but in a way he didn't. I'd suspected for a long time that something was wrong, and so had my mom. We'd all pretended nothing was happening, until the day came when we couldn't pretend.

In sixth grade, Mr. Dong was my science teacher. At first, I didn't do much more than laugh at his name. But in October, I started listening to him, and he got me interested in science. I joined his science club, and my dad and I built wooden mazes for the classroom rats. Once the mazes were built, I came up with a series of experiments to figure out how quickly rats learn. I put different food rewards at the end of the runs, and I changed the difficulty level of the mazes. I timed the rats and made graphs in Excel. Other teachers came and judged the projects, and I took first place, beating out Anya Lin, who usually won everything.

When my parents found out I'd get a medal at an evening assembly, they insisted that we go. The chess club, the math club, the band, and the orchestra also gave out awards that night. Science club was last. After what seemed like forever, Mr. Dong took the podium. Before handing out awards, he talked about the great future that awaited all of us. My medal looked like one of those chocolate coins wrapped in gold paper you can get at

Trader Joe's, but it felt good to hear Mr. Dong say "Brock Ripley" and to look out and see a roomful of people clapping for me.

After the awards ceremony, we walked back to the Honda. My mom was telling me how proud she was, but my dad stayed quiet. I didn't think much of his silence; over the past months, he'd become quieter and quieter.

When we reached the car, I climbed into the back seat, while Mom slipped into the front passenger seat. We sat as my dad stood outside, his hand on the car door. We waited for about a minute, wondering why he didn't just open the door and climb in. Finally, my mom reached over and pressed the button that lowered the window. "Is something wrong?"

My dad's voice was shaky. "My hand—it's sort of locked."

My mom got out, moved around to the driver's side, and helped him open his hand up. As she did, I heard him whisper, "What's happening to me?"

CHAPTER 3

After that, things changed rapidly. Besides being a soccer player, my dad had been a middle distance runner at Eastern Washington — the two mile was his race. For as long as I could remember, he'd run thirty minutes every morning, and when he neared our house he would sprint the final one hundred yards, his legs firing like pistons. I was always the fastest kid in my class for fifty yards, but after that I grabbed my side and was done. He was powerful in a way I hoped someday to be.

In the weeks following the awards ceremony, he'd go out to run only to come back after a few minutes. He'd sit on the sofa and rub his legs. When I asked him what was wrong, he'd say he was fine, but by the middle of summer he'd stopped running entirely.

In the summer, it stays light in Seattle until almost ten at night. Most evenings, I hung out with my friends, but if nothing was doing with them, my dad had always been willing to go to the park after dinner and kick around a soccer ball.

But that summer, he changed. His back was stiff . . . his leg hurt . . . he had work to do for the bank. After he'd turned me down a half-dozen times, I stopped asking. Soon, he wasn't able to prune the hedges in the backyard, mow the lawn, or lift heavy packages.

My dad and I both have dark hair and eyes. In the summer, both of us get deep tans. He stayed pale that year, and his eyes lost color, changing from dark brown to gray. He drove differently, too. He'd always been a fast driver, looking to beat the light by cutting in front of drivers who were going too slowly for him. Now he poked along in the far right lane, his foot resting on the brake.

He hardly ate, and he went from looking strong to looking skinny. Mom wanted him to go to the doctor; I heard them arguing when I was upstairs in my room and they were down in the kitchen.

Right before school started again, my mom gave me the news. "Your father is going to spend a couple of days in the hospital. They're going to run tests to find out why he isn't feeling well. Don't worry, though. They'll get him the right medicine and everything will be fine."

I believed her. I was certain the doctors would figure out what was wrong and make him right. But when my dad came home two days later, he called me into the kitchen, had me sit down in a chair across from him, and told me he had something called Steinert's disease. "My muscles stiffen up quickly, and they twitch when they shouldn't. I'm losing strength."

"But medicine can make you better, right?"

He frowned. "Maybe someday, but not today." He forced himself to smile. "That's the bad news. But there's good news too. This disease progresses slowly. I'm going to live for a long, long time. So for someone who is really unlucky, I'm actually very lucky. There are people who have it a lot worse, so I'm not going to feel sorry for myself. And I don't want you to feel sorry for me either. Okay?"

CHAPTER 4

There were five of us at Gilman Park on the day that Hunter Gates appeared. Five guys aren't enough for a real soccer game, so we did what we always did when we were short-handed—I stood in goal, and the other guys took turns firing shots at me from about twenty yards out. I'd been the goalkeeper for the Whitman Middle School team, so I was in goal at Gilman.

When I'd first played for Whitman, I was a right forward. My speed made me a threat. When one of our fullbacks booted the ball downfield, my job was to outrun everybody to the ball. As long as I avoided being offside, I'd be able to score goals on a regular basis.

That was Coach Nelson's strategy, but it never panned out. I don't know why, but I can't settle a ball without coming to a complete stop, or close to it. That gave defenders time to catch up, and once it became a battle for the ball, I lost. I was never good at the elbowing and pushing part of soccer. Same thing with wrestling or fighting for rebounds in basketball. I wanted to be a guy who left some skin in the game, but when it came to it, I always pulled back. "Toughen up, Brock!" Coach Nelson would holler. But time after time, I'd have the ball taken away. Coach Nelson would throw his head back in agony; the parents of the other kids would groan; my teammates would glare.

In seventh grade, Coach Nelson put Alan Page out on the wing and stuck me on the bench. Alan isn't nearly as fast as I am, so he didn't break free often. But when he got the ball, he fought off defenders, and his shots sometimes found the back of the net. Once he took my spot, I wandered the sidelines, one of the useless guys.

Then I caught a break. Early in the eighth grade season, Trevin Winehart, our goalie, didn't show up for a game. Coach Nelson looked long and hard over his bench players before pointing at me. "Brock, get in the goal." That game, I stopped every shot—okay, none of them were too hard—and we won 2–0. Winehart came back, but I'd become the Whitman goalkeeper.

With me as keeper, our team clicked. On offense, somebody would sneak a goal or two across, and on defense I'd stop whatever shots came my way.

For the first weeks of our winning streak, I thought

I was a natural goalkeeper. Good hands, quick reactions, foot speed—I had it all. Then came the game against Jane Addams Middle School.

Those guys were rough right from the start. One of their forwards, a stocky guy with blond hair, always looked for a chance to give me a little shot with his forearm when the ref wasn't looking. Coach Nelson had warned us about them beforehand. "Don't let these guys intimidate you. They hit you, you hit them back harder."

The McDermotts and those guys dished out as much as they took. I wanted to be tough like the McDermotts, tough like everybody else. But the blond guy kept hitting me every chance he got, and I never made him pay. *Next time, I'll show him.* That's what I told myself, but the next time was just like every other time.

Still, we were winning, ahead 1–0 with only a few minutes left in the game. That's when Addams got lucky. I didn't see exactly what happened, but the ball somehow popped loose at midfield, the blond guy took off down the sideline, and a long kick led him perfectly.

Before I could even swallow, he was bearing down on me with a full head of steam, his legs eating up ground. He wasn't trying to deke me either; he was coming right at me, intent on rolling right over me.

I knew what to do: charge him, cut down on his angle, and make him take a difficult shot under pressure. I took a step forward, and then fear paralyzed me. He suddenly seemed huge. I took a step back, then another, and I tripped and fell. He roared by me and drilled a shot into the net while I lay on the ground like a beetle that had been flipped onto its back.

That's when I heard the whistle. I looked to the assistant ref along the sideline, and his flag was up. The blond kid had been offside. His goal was waved off, and a few minutes later we were celebrating another victory.

Nobody said anything to me about my collapse, but Coach Nelson, my teammates, and the parents had seen it. The parents of the Addams kids had seen it. So had the referees. They all knew I'd gone gutless. My fear hadn't cost us the victory, but it could have. And that fear was still there—like a sickness deep inside that's become quiet but is still lurking, sure to come back.

At night, I kept having the same dream—the blond guy would charge hard at me, my legs would tangle themselves, and I'd fall, giving away both the goal and the game. I'd see the players and parents laughing at me, pointing and laughing, just as Hunter and his friends had laughed at Jerry Jerzek. I'd wake up in a sweat, my heart pounding, my body shaking.

Over the next weeks, our victories kept coming, but I couldn't enjoy them. An hour before each game, my head would start swimming and my stomach would turn over.

If my dad hadn't been sick, he'd have taken me to

Gilman Park and had me stand in the goal while he dribbled toward me. He'd have started out slowly and then picked up his speed little by little, easing me along, letting me get used to the speed of the game. He'd have given me tips on when to charge and when to back off.

He wanted to do all those things and more; I could see it in his eyes. But with the way things were, I had no one. I was so panicky before games that I'd sneak behind the laurel hedge in our backyard and puke, our neighbor's insane beagle barking at me as I retched.

My dad came to all my games. That was tough. I *wanted* him at the games, but I *didn't want* him. Driving was getting harder for him. He was afraid that he wouldn't be able to brake quickly, so he drove like an old lady. When people honked, his face turned bright red.

Just standing on the sidelines during a game was a struggle for him. My dad was stable when he used his arm braces, but he hated using them in public. He'd find something to lean against during the game, and he'd sit in the car at the break. By the end of every game, his face was gray.

He insisted warm weather would help, but warm weather didn't come. The calendar said late April, but for two straight weeks every day was cold and rainy. We had three games during that stretch and he'd been at each of them, looking older and weaker. We'd won all three games, and I'd hated all three games.

As I ate breakfast on the Saturday morning of our next game, I looked out at the dark clouds. The game was at noon, and it would be pouring by then. I pictured my dad leaning against a chainlink fence, the wind whipping the rain into his face, the wet and cold seeping into what was left of his muscles.

He came into the kitchen as I was finishing my toast. "You don't have to come today," I said, trying to sound casual. "I can catch a ride with the McDermotts."

He knew right away. His jaw clenched, and his neck reddened. He started to say something, then stopped. "I'll think about it," he said at last.

In the end, he stayed home.

After that, an hour before every game Mr. McDermott pulled his black SUV into our driveway and honked. I'd hop in the back and be off. The first couple of times, I worried that Rory or Tim would ask why my dad had stopped coming to the games, but neither did.

After each game, I told my dad about every play I made, so he wouldn't feel he was missing anything. Usually I made up one save where I'd fought off some attacker right in front of the goal. My dad would always look hard at me then, his eyes sizing me up.

CHAPTER 5

We beat Eckstein 3–1 to win the North Division, putting us into the city championship against Mercer Middle School, the champions of the South. I figured I'd ride with the McDermotts to the Mercer game, but on the day of the game—a warm May night—my dad told me he'd take me.

"You don't have to go," I said. "I can tell you about it."

He waved me off. "My son is playing in a championship game—I want to see it."

An hour before we left, with the beagle barking like a mad dog, I threw up behind our bushes. Usually that made me feel better, but that day I still felt weak and dizzy. The game was across town in West Seattle, thirty minutes away. My mom was anxious too. "Are you sure?" she asked as my dad picked up the keys and headed to the car. My mom made it to some games, but my dad didn't miss a single one.

"I'll be fine," my dad said.

We didn't talk much on the drive. He had his right foot resting on the brake, and his eyes were unnaturally wide open. Beads of sweat lined his forehead.

He used side roads the whole way, driving through Harbor Island instead of using the West Seattle Bridge. When we finally pulled into the parking lot at West Seattle Stadium, I opened the car door and stepped out, but my dad stayed in the driver's seat. "I'll watch from the car," he said, leaning toward me. "I know it's a little odd, but—"

"That's fine," I said, cutting him off. "You'll see better anyway."

As I went through the pregame routine with my teammates, I was afraid someone would ask why my dad was sitting in the car, but no one did. That's one thing I've learned: you think people are watching you, noticing things, but they're not.

Minutes later, we were on the field, playing for the city championship. I jumped up and touched the crossbar for good luck, and then I looked to the parking lot. I spotted my dad's car and gave him a small wave. I thought I saw him wave back.

During the first few minutes, a couple of long, soft shots came my way. They were exactly what I needed—some action to stay loose, but not so much action that I felt under siege.

We dominated the first half, so most of the time the ball was on the Mercer side of the field, seventy yards away from me. I tried to stay focused, but with the ball so far away, my mind kept going to my father. Occasionally, I'd peek over at the Honda, sad to think of him sitting in the dark in the car, his whole body hurting.

Even though we put pressure on Mercer, we had only one good shot—by Alan Page—but his kick sailed wide. At the half, the score was 0–0. As I ate orange sections during the break, I glanced over to the parking lot. The Honda wasn't there. Then, before I had time to panic, I spotted it. My dad had moved to the other end of the field so that he'd be able to see me after we switched sides. I gave him a wave, and again I thought I saw his hand come up.

Before the start of the second half, Coach Nelson told us to take more chances. "You've got to *win* a championship; they don't fall in your lap." The other guys cheered, but not me. If we took more chances, then Mercer would have more chances—it was as simple as that.

The Mercer coach must have given a similar talk to his team, because early in the second half both sides made rush after rush. Tim McDermott, playing his best game of the year, saved me twice, but on three shots it was all me. The first one I punched wide; on the second I laid out for a bullet headed toward the left corner. I deflected it, but the ball caromed right to a Mercer guy. If he hadn't hurried his shot, he could have scored easily. But instead of taking his time and putting the ball into the corner of the net, he blasted a point-blank shot at my head. I deflected the ball up and over the crossbar. On our side, parents cheered like crazy. Those were the best saves I'd ever made, even if the third one was pure luck.

That's when the fantasy came, or the voodoo, or whatever it was. I decided that if we won that game, then my dad would get better. But if we lost the game, then he'd get worse. It was stupid, and I knew it was stupid, but that's what I thought.

After the flurry of scoring chances on both sides, a long stretch of nothing followed, with the ball stuck near midfield. As the time ticked away, the aggressiveness disappeared on both sides. I saw the referee look down at his watch. There couldn't have been more than a couple of minutes left. We were headed to a shootout.

Right then, one of the Mercer forwards took a perfect cross-field pass, settled the ball, and put a spin move on Rory McDermott. Rory slipped and fell, and suddenly the Mercer guy was coming at me, with no defenders back.

It was my nightmare, only now it was real. I tried to charge, but when I'd taken a few steps, I froze. The Mercer guy kept coming, getting bigger and moving faster. I took a panicky step backward, realized it was too late to retreat. Finally, I turned sideways to avoid being hit, the way you step aside when a bicyclist flies by on the street. A second later, the ball was past me.

The Mercer guy didn't have to boom the ball, not after my blunder. He just needed to be accurate. I watched the ball as it bounced along, tumbling forward over the bumpy turf, torturing me. And then the ball was in the net, and the Mercer guys were running around the field, their arms high in celebration, and my Whitman teammates were staring at me, wondering why I'd backed off when I'd needed to challenge.

After the game, the Mercer players got trophies and we got cheap red ribbons. As we trudged off the field, Coach Nelson gave me a pat on the back. "Don't blame yourself," he said, but I knew that at the biggest moment I'd wimped out.

On the drive home—another struggle for my dad—neither of us mentioned the goal. When we reached the house, I had to help him out of the driver's seat, and he leaned on me as he labored up the porch stairs that led to the front door.

CHAPTER [illegible]

That summer day at Gilman Park, while I was in goal and my friends blasted shots at me, I'd sneak looks at Hunter Gates and his father. Hunter's dad was the same age, stood the same height, and had the same build as my father. Both had dark hair that was going gray and salt-and-pepper goatees. But there was nothing stiff or tired or weak about Hunter's dad. He moved the way my father used to move—with power.

We took a break, all of us sprawling out in the shade of a maple tree by the fence. We talked mostly about high school, guessing what Crown Hill High would be like, wondering how the scary older kids like Hunter would treat us.

We'd been lying around on the grass for ten minutes when Hunter's dad called out. "You, in the Sounders shirt. The kid who was playing goalie. Come here for a minute, okay?"

I'd been watching them, but I couldn't believe that they'd been watching me. I pointed my finger at my chest. "Me?"

"Just for a few minutes. We need a wide receiver." My friends gaped at me. Hunter Gates was going to throw passes to me.

I stood, brushed the grass off the seat of my pants, and jogged over. Hunter's father stuck out his hand and I shook it. "My name is Bill Gates, but I'm not that Bill Gates. What's your name?"

"Brock Ripley," I answered, pretending not to know him or Hunter, though everybody in the Ballard neighborhood of Seattle knew both of them.

He motioned toward his son. "That's my son, Hunter." I looked over; Hunter waved at me, a wave that said, *Let's see what you've got.*

Hunter looked like he could have been in the movies, maybe in something like *Fast and Furious 12.* He had shoulder-length blond hair, brown eyes, and brown eyebrows. His jaw was straight and strong, with the beginnings of a beard. He was wearing a muscle shirt, and he had a tattoo of a snake on his right biceps. He looked like what he was—a star quarterback.

"I saw you in goal," Mr. Gates said. "You've got soft hands and you're quick. Can you catch a football?"

* * *

It was simple. I was to run seven steps straight out, then turn quickly to the right and expect to see a football coming at me.

Mr. Gates raised his hand. "Ready?"

I nodded.

"Go!"

I did what he said, but the instant I looked back the ball was on me, flying as if it had been shot out of a cannon. The football ripped through my hands, bending back my right thumb. I howled in pain as the ball bounded crazily behind me.

Hunter looked disgustedly at the sky and then turned to his father and shook his head. I felt as if I'd suddenly ceased to exist. I didn't have to look over to know that my friends were snickering. "He's useless," Hunter said to his father.

Mr. Gates nodded and then waved me away. "Go on back to your buddies. Thanks, though."

"I can catch," I said, the anger in my voice masking a humiliation so great that I was on the verge of tears. "I just wasn't ready— " I stopped and composed my voice. "Give me another try."

Mr. Gates cocked his head, uncertain. "A football could break your nose, and you don't look like you've played the game."

"I can do it."

He glanced at Hunter, who shrugged.

"All right. We'll give it another try," Mr. Gates said.

I lined up to the right, my nerves on high alert. I didn't want to start high school with Hunter Gates pointing me out to his friends as a loser and having the whole bunch of them turn me into the next Jerry Jumper. I could not drop a second pass.

I raced out seven yards, made the cut, looked back. The ball was right in my face, with the same velocity as before. My aching thumb screamed at me, but I caught that ball and held on.

Mr. Gates smiled, surprised. "That's the way, kid."

I turned to Hunter Gates, and he nodded—a nod of respect.

I caught Hunter's bullets—or at least most of them—for the next twenty minutes, my thumb throbbing the whole time. After about ten minutes, Tim McDermott called out to me. "We're going, Brock. See you tomorrow."

I wanted to leave too, but leaving wasn't possible, not until Hunter and his father told me I could leave. That's how it was with them.

Eventually, Hunter's arm tired and his passes lost velocity, which was fine with me, because I was winded and my thumb was swelling. Mr. Gates waved his hands. "That's enough for today." Hunter started packing up their gear; his father came over to me.

"Are you in high school?"

"I'll be a freshman at Crown Hill High."

"Have you thought about playing football?"

I sort of twitched. "Not really."

"Well, think it over. Hunter is the QB at Crown. All the starting receivers on last year's team graduated, so the position is wide open. You've got speed and great hands, especially for someone who has never played." He paused, then spoke again. "What's your dad do, Brock?"

"He's a loan officer at SeaRock Bank."

"Is he a sports guy? Do you think you could get him to throw a football to you?"

Mr. Gates stood in front of me, muscular, bursting with health. Hunter had his back to me, but he was close. I didn't want him to hear. I didn't want him making fun of me or my dad. I lowered my voice. "My father has been sick recently, but when he gets better he'll throw to me."

Mr. Gates beamed. "That's great. The more balls you catch, the better. With those hands, that speed, and Hunter throwing the ball, you could be a star." He winked. "Girls go for wide receivers. You'd have your pick."

CHAPTER 7

I spent the walk home trying to sort out my thoughts. I'd always fantasized about being a football star—what guy hasn't? Now Mr. Gates was telling me that I actually could be a football player. I didn't want people to hear my name and then immediately think of my failure in the final minute of the Mercer game. Football might be a way to get out from under that.

All Seattle public high schools play their games at Memorial Stadium in Seattle Center. I pictured myself on that old field, catching a perfect Hunter Gates spiral, fighting through tacklers, and plowing my way into the end zone.

Then I came back to reality. As my father had grown weaker, my mom had become more protective. She was always warning me to stay away from kids who did drugs or drank. If I rode my bicycle, she insisted I wear a helmet. During soccer season, she even told me not to head the ball. When I gave her a *You've got to be kidding* look, her lips turned down into a scowl. "For your information, heading the ball can cause a concussion. That's a brain injury, Brock. A brain injury."

My father watched the UW Huskies on Saturday and the Seahawks on Sunday. He was a good athlete, so he might have played on his high school team. If he did, he never talked about it.

If he hadn't been sick, I could have told him that I needed to prove myself to *myself,* and he'd have understood. But, every week, he was spending more time alone, and it was my mom who made the decisions. How could I get her to understand?

The late-afternoon sun shone down; the sky was blue and clear. When I reached my house, I still had no plan. But football tryouts were still a month away. An idea was sure to come to me.

After dinner, I played Minecraft online with Rory and Tim until both of them had to quit. Then I did a search for "Hunter Gates." The top site was Recruits.com. I clicked and was taken to a list of the best quarterback prospects in the country. I kept scrolling down until I finally found Hunter at number ninety-two. Next to his name was a short summary.

Took a step back as sophomore. Unproven.

Beside his name was a red arrow pointing down.

CHAPTER 6

That summer, I was at Gilman Park nearly every day. Hunter Gates and his dad showed up about half the time. Hunter would stretch for a few minutes, and then his father would supervise while he did agility drills and ran wind sprints. Once he was loose, Hunter would throw the ball to his father, who scrutinized every movement.

Eventually, Mr. Gates's eyes would look around the playing field, and I'd step away from my buddies. "We need you for a little bit, kid," he'd say, his hand motioning for me to join them. Sometimes he'd even say "Brock."

Mainly we worked on the slant pattern. Mr. Gates insisted I get the footwork perfect so that Hunter could get his timing right. "To run a good slant," Mr. Gates explained, "you take three steps and then cut hard on your outside foot. Do it right, and the cornerback will be tripping over his own feet."

Again and again, I'd run about five yards and then

cut at a sharp angle toward the center of the field. Hunter would fire the ball to me, and I'd catch it. There was nothing much to it that I could see, but when I told Mr. Gates that, he snorted. "What you're doing now hardly counts. Making the catch when there's a linebacker or a safety about to unload on you—that's when you'll find out if you're a player."

Once Hunter and I had the timing of the slant down, we switched to the out. I'd drive up the field five yards and then make a sharp cut toward the sideline. "You won't have to worry about hanging on after being hit on this one," Mr. Gates said. "The pass will carry you to the sideline. Just be sure to get a foot down before you step out of bounds."

At first, I ran the route like a robot, counting my steps, watching my plant foot. Then, somehow, I didn't have to. I had my back to Hunter, so I couldn't see him, but I knew when his arm was raised, knew when he'd released the ball, knew when to turn. I could tell from his eyes that he knew what I was going to do before I did.

Quarterbacks and receivers work hard to get that kind of feel for each other. Sometimes it never comes, no matter how much work they put in. But Hunter and I had it. I don't know why or how; I just know that we did. It was as if our minds were synched.

CHAPTER 9

One day in July, a Chinese kid about my age came traipsing across the field with his parents. I'd seen him before, running down my block in the morning. He was shorter than me, but stockier. He wasn't a sprinter, but a middle distance guy. Like my father, he looked as if he could run through a wall.

There are a million better places to have a picnic in Seattle than Gilman Park, but the kid and his parents carried a couple of baskets over to a ratty picnic bench near the chainlink fence. The kid's mother spread out a tablecloth and soon they were using chopsticks to eat from the white takeout containers you get at Chinese restaurants.

After a short time, the kid's father started shouting in a high-pitched, angry voice, noodles hanging out of his mouth. His wife, who was dressed in black except for a red bandanna about her head, lowered her eyes. She took a few bites of her food, but within minutes the father was at her again, waving his chopsticks around while talking fast. The whole thing was so strange that it was impossible not to stare.

A bunch of guys who looked about twenty—shirts off, jeans sagging, cigarettes dangling from their lips—wandered from the street onto the field. They were either high or pretending to be high—shoving one another, fake fighting, dropping f-bombs left and right.

When they spotted the Chinese kid and his parents, big smiles came to their faces. The kid's father had started yelling again, ordering his wife to eat, and shoving food into his mouth as if he was demonstrating to her how it was done. The saggy-jeans guys started mimicking the father, pretending to gobble from imaginary bowls, loudly sucking up imaginary noodles. They bowed mockingly to one another, hands joined as if in prayer.

I started to turn away—who wants to see stuff like that?—but out of the corner of my eye I saw the Chinese kid jump to his feet. When I looked back, he was up in the faces of those guys, telling them to go away. They were laughing at him, sticking their teeth out and pretending to speak Chinese. The kid's father was yelling for him to come back to the table; his mother started crying.

The Chinese kid looked back to his parents, and in that split second, one of the guys stuck his foot behind the kid and shoved him. The kid went flying back, falling hard. He got up and charged the guy who had tripped him. But as he ran at him, one of the other guys stuck his foot out and the kid went down again, this time face first.

"I call the police!" the father screamed as he held up his cell phone, and at those words the guys took off, looking back and laughing as they half ran, half walked away.

The Chinese kid got up and started back to the picnic table. As he walked, he looked over at me. For a moment, our eyes caught and held, and then he dropped his head. I turned away and went back to kicking the soccer ball around.

A few minutes later, the mother gathered up all the picnic stuff and put it back in the basket. They left then, the Chinese kid staring at the grass as he walked back to his car.

That was the first time I saw Richie Fang get shoved around for no reason, but it wasn't the last. And it wasn't the last time that he'd fight back, either.

Hunter Gates didn't show up that day, so I was home early. When I stepped inside my house, my dad was sitting in a rocking chair in the front room reading the main section of the *Seattle Times.* I said hello, and then my eye stopped on the photo at the top of the business section that was on the coffee table in front of him. Mr. Gates's face was staring at me.

My dad noticed. "Something wrong?"

I pointed to the newspaper. "That's Mr. Gates, right?"

My father nodded. "Sure is. And he'll be public enemy number one around here for a while."

"Why?"

"He's the lead attorney for the company pushing to run oil and coal trains to Cherry Point. Everybody hates the idea."

"Why's he doing it, then?"

"He's a lawyer; it's his job." My father paused. "You know his son, right? Hunter, the quarterback."

"I know who he is, but I don't really know him. Some days, I see him at Gilman Park throwing the football around with his dad."

"They're at Gilman? That surprises me. I figured his kid would be at some NFL-sponsored football camp. I guess his father has to stay around here to work on the lawsuits."

It was the perfect opportunity to tell my dad that I wanted to try out for football, but I couldn't bring the words out. There's still time, I told myself.

CHAPTER 10

And then time ran out.

One day in early August, after I'd finished running patterns and Hunter was headed to the car, Mr. Gates handed me a packet of papers—the forms for football. "Get your mom or dad to fill these out," he said, and then he stopped. "How is your dad? Doing better?"

"He's a little better," I lied.

"Good," Mr. Gates said. "Glad to hear it." Then he tapped the papers he'd handed me. "Tryouts are in two weeks. You can't participate unless these papers are signed and your medical forms are up to date. I'll be helping out with quarterbacks and wide receivers. I'm a volunteer, not a paid coach, but you'll have somebody in your corner."

"Dad, let's go," Hunter called out. "I'm hungry."

Mr. Gates looked over. "In a minute." He turned

back to me. "I don't suppose you've heard of Renaldo Nehemiah, have you?"

I shook my head.

"Nehemiah was a track star, a world-class athlete. When his track career ended, he turned to football. For a few years, he was a deep threat for the 49ers. I can see you being the Renaldo Nehemiah of the Crown Hill High team. You've got the speed and you've got the hands"—he stopped and motioned with his head toward Hunter—"and you've got somebody who can get you the ball."

After dinner that night, I followed my dad out of the kitchen. He had a new chair in the living room. It looked like a regular chair, but it came with a remote that let him raise and lower it, making it easier for him to get in and out. He kept a blanket over the arm so that no one could see the control panel, but there was no covering the hum of the machinery. It wasn't until he was settled in his chair that he even noticed I'd followed him. "Got a minute?" I asked.

"Of course. What's on your mind?"

Sitting on the sofa across from him, I took a deep breath and the words rushed out. I told him about working out with Hunter Gates under the eye of his father. "I know I've never played football," I said, "but practicing with Hunter has changed me. Running routes and catching passes—it's a million times better than playing goalie. I want to give football a try, but I need you to sign the permission forms. So, would you sign them for me?"

When I finished, the room fell quiet. "No, Brock," he said, breaking the silence. "No."

My body went cold. "Why not?'

He ran his hand over his mouth a few times and then leaned forward. "Brock, you know why not. And it's not just concussions. It's knees, ribs, shoulders, ankles, hips. Football is brutal."

"It isn't all that different from soccer, and you let me play that. I'm not going to be a lineman or a running back. I'll be a wide receiver."

"When wide receivers go over the middle, they take harder hits than anyone. And with your speed, the coach is sure to put you on special teams too. Those guys race downfield on kickoffs and punts. Nothing is more dangerous than that."

I felt a wave of desperation. I hadn't realized how much I wanted to play football until I could see the chance slipping away. "This is high school football, Dad. Not the Seahawks. Guys don't hit that hard. Besides, I want to prove to myself that I can do it."

"Do what?"

I felt my body slump. I breathed out, slowly. "You know. Make the team. Play."

He looked at me for a while. "Stick with soccer, Brock. It's safer, and you're good at it."

"I'm *not* good at it. I don't even *play* soccer. Not really. I stand in goal and watch everybody else play. I'm bored out of my mind ninety-nine percent of the time. But when Hunter Gates throws the football to me — that's great. Sometimes I — "

He interrupted me. "The answer is no."

"So you won't listen? What I think doesn't matter?"

"On this topic, no."

"Fine," I snapped, and then stomped upstairs to my room, flopped on my bed, and opened my laptop. I logged on to Halo and played on autopilot, my mind raging.

I'd been playing for about an hour when I heard a light tap on my door. I was sure it was my mom, but when I opened up, my dad was in front of me. It was hard for him to get upstairs, so I felt guilty the moment I saw him.

"Can I come in?"

"Sure," I said. I reached for my desk chair. "Do you want to sit down?"

"No, I'll stand. I won't be long." His eyes caught the computer screen. "Go on. Get to a good place to stop. I don't want to spoil your game."

I shook my head. "I'm done." I turned and hit the escape key, not bothering to save.

I turned back to face him.

"You know I wish I could do more with you."

My throat felt as if it were filled with gauze. "It's okay. I don't mind."

He laughed, a joyless laugh. "Well, I mind. I mind a lot."

He looked at his hands and then opened and closed his fingers three or four times, an exercise I'd seen him do often. His eyes came back to me. "Playing football is important?"

"I want to play. I think I can be good, and I want the challenge."

"You'd be way behind the other players. You'd be one of the few guys, maybe the only guy, who has never played on a team, never been tackled, never thrown a block. You'll probably end up on the freshman team, not the varsity."

I shrugged. Mr. Gates had just about begged me to try out. Why would he do that if he thought I couldn't make varsity? "I just want to give it a try."

My father stared at me for a long time. When he spoke again, his voice was businesslike. "Okay, here's the deal. They say coaches are teaching safer ways to play the game. But if you get a concussion—that's it. No more football. You understand?"

My heart was pounding. "Are you saying that I can play?"

"You can play."

"But what about Mom?"

"I talked to her. She thinks it's a stupid macho male thing, but she won't stop you."

"The concussion rule is her idea?"

My dad shook his head. "No. The concussion rule is *our* idea. If you don't accept that condition, I'm not signing. So what do you say?"

PART TWO

CHAPTER

The first thing that surprised me about the tryouts was the number of guys on the field. There must have been a hundred—ranging in height from five two to six seven and in weight from one hundred twenty to three hundred.

It was a hot summer day for Seattle, over eighty. The head coach was an older guy with a scary name: Coach Payne. He looked like he'd been coaching for a century. Guys said that this was going to be his last year.

Coach Payne positioned himself on top of a tower and used a bullhorn to give directions to the assistant coaches and parent volunteers who directed the small groups.

We started with stretches that morphed into pushups, sit-ups, and jumping jacks. Next came agility drills. Up . . . down . . . left . . . right . . . forward . . . backward—all with coaches and volunteers screaming at us to go faster and push harder. I didn't see a football until an hour had passed.

Mr. Gates had told me that he'd work with the receivers, but he spent ninety-nine percent of his time with Hunter. Mr. Laurence, a young guy with long blond hair and tattoos of barbed wire running up his arms onto his neck, directed the receivers. He seemed more like a Hells Angel than a football coach. I felt so lost that I thought about gliding over to the side of the field, waiting for a moment when no one was looking, and then slipping away. But I couldn't quit, not after begging my dad to sign.

There were nine receivers in all. The freshmen were about my size. The other five guys weren't particularly taller than me, but they were muscular and had stubbly beards. My arms looked like twigs compared with theirs.

Mr. Gates and Mr. Laurence directed the passing drills together. Hunter had more velocity than the other two quarterbacks, and I was the best at hanging on to his passes. My sure-handedness was ticking off the returning receivers, especially Colton Sparks, a junior with strange green eyes who'd been Hunter's best friend since middle school.

After twenty minutes, Mr. Gates took the quarterbacks to the other side of the field, while Mr. Laurence had us follow him to the end zone. "Make a circle," he commanded, and when we did he threw a towel onto the ground. "I know who can play catch. Now I want to find out who can play football."

It didn't take long to figure out the drill, if you could call it a drill. It was a one-on-one tug of war, but instead of pulling a rope you pulled a towel. Colton snatched the towel and shoved it in my face. "Okay, you little wuss, get out here."

He took hold; I took hold. Mr. Laurence, his eyes excited, blew his whistle. Instantly, Colton was dragging me across the field. I thought my arms were going to come out of their sockets. Finally, Colton pulled me across some line I didn't even know was there. When Mr. Laurence blew his whistle, Colton let go of the towel and I went flying back, landing on my butt. Colton stood over me, grinning down, while the other guys shrieked with laughter.

Since I'd lost, I had to challenge somebody and pull again. I picked Ty Erdman, a five-foot-six guy with short arms and short legs. I thought I could beat him, but he was like a bulldog. That contest was over fast too.

My shoulders burned, but I had to stay in the center until I beat somebody. Mr. Laurence enjoyed my humiliation as much as the other guys, grinning and shouting, *"Pull! Pull! Pull!"*

After I'd lost my fourth straight, my muscles were twitching and I was gasping for breath. Mr. Laurence told me to sit down, which I did, salty sweat dripping into my eyes. Other guys pulled the towel then. I dropped my head between my knees and stared at the grass.

Finally, the bullhorn's siren wailed.

All the groups reassembled at the north end zone. Coach Payne's voice boomed out. "You're going to be tired and sore tomorrow. That's football. You go through pain to reach victory. We'll have two sessions starting Thursday. Be here, on time, ready to go. Dismissed."

As I walked off the field, Colton sidled up next to me. "Not such a big deal after all, are you?"

"At least I can catch a football," I shot back.

He snorted. "You won't catch anything when there's a safety waiting to lay you out. You don't have the stones to play this game."

My mind was ablaze as I walked home. Colton Sparks could win all the towel pulls in the world, but that wouldn't change the fact that I could catch passes that he dropped. And I wasn't afraid of being tackled by a safety or a linebacker. Sparks could take that stupid towel, wrap it around his neck, and hang himself with it.

CHAPTER 2

Two-a-days started, and every day was more grueling than the day before. Each session ended with the same stupid towel pull. I was always the big winner when it came to catching passes and the big loser in the towel pull.

On Monday afternoon of the second week, we put on shoulder pads and a helmet for the first time. I wanted to love the pads and the helmet, but with all those straps and plastic flaps, I couldn't move my arms freely, so I wasn't able to adjust quickly to the ball. And with a heavy hunk of plastic and foam surrounding my head, I had trouble seeing. I'd race out on a fly pattern, or make a quick cut on a down-and-out, look back, and not find the ball. The magic I'd had with Hunter disappeared. His passes were hitting the ground in front of me, behind me, to my left and right. Hunter would scowl at me and shake his head, and I saw Mr. Laurence look up to the sky in disbelief. I fell like a rock, from top receiver to middle of the pack to bottom guy. Colton Sparks and the older guys enjoyed every second of it.

The final day of tryouts wasn't a tryout at all — it was a game. I knew if I didn't play great, I'd be stuck on the freshman team.

As I lay in bed the night before the scrimmage, I thought through the next day. I was starting to get used to the helmet and shoulder pads. I just needed everything to come together. I pictured myself streaking down the sideline, hauling in a perfect strike from Hunter, making a nifty move to get past the safety, and taking it to the house.

A touchdown would shut Colton and the rest of them up.

I ran through different versions of that play, and then I must have fallen asleep, because the next thing I knew it was morning.

When I got downstairs, my parents had already finished breakfast and were heading out — my dad to his job at Sea Rock Bank and my mom to her job at Metro Transit.

What to eat? I didn't want to puke after the first hit, but I didn't want to run out of gas either. I decided on yogurt, a blueberry muffin, and a bowl of Cheerios. Enough, but not too much.

At nine thirty, I walked to the practice field. I thought

I'd be one of the first there, but when I climbed the stairs to the field I saw about sixty guys stretching out, tossing footballs around—all itching to go. I spotted Hunter and nodded to him. He surprised me by nodding back.

The coaches had divided us into teams—Red and Black. Mine was the third name called out for the Red team. After that, I listened intently for Hunter's name. With all the bad luck I'd been having, I was afraid he'd be on the Black team, but he was on the Red team as well. That explained the earlier nod. I was still his best chance for a long TD strike, and he knew it.

Coach Payne gave us a talk about hitting hard but hitting safely, too. "No head shots. You go high and you're off the field."

I was flanked way out on the right side for the opening kickoff. My assignment was to race downfield, staying in my lane, and force the runner to the middle, where a swarm of guys were waiting.

My heart was thumping; my ears were ringing. Coach Payne blew his whistle and our kicker, Danny Ingram, booted the ball. It wasn't much of a kick—the kicking game was the weakest part of the team—neither high nor deep.

The ball was headed to the opposite side of the field. I raced over that way, hoping to be able to pile on at the end of the tackle so I could get the feel of contact. But then—just like that—the return man pitched the ball to a guy coming around on a reverse. Instead of moving away from me, the whole world was suddenly headed right at me.

I was looking for the ball carrier, which is why I never saw J'Varre Dixon. But J'Varre saw me. He measured me like a lumberjack measures a tree, and then he leveled me with a shot to the ribs. A millisecond later, I was lying flat on my back, gasping for air like a fish on the sidewalk.

Somebody must have tackled the runner or forced him out of bounds, because I heard a whistle ending the play. J'Varre stood over me, grinning. Then I heard a second whistle. "No taunting! That would cost us fifteen yards in a game!" Coach Payne shouted.

J'Varre turned and raced to his side of the field, high-fiving guys as he went. I wobbled over to the sideline, found the bench, dropped my head toward my knees, and tried to keep from throwing up.

I felt a hand on my shoulder and heard Coach Payne's voice. With him was Mr. Rosen, the team trainer. "You okay, kid?" Mr. Rosen asked.

"Yeah, I'm okay."

"Your head clear?"

"My head's fine. He hit me in the gut."

Mr. Rosen shone a light in my eyes and had me answer some questions. With each passing second, I felt better. Mr. Rosen turned to Coach Payne, who'd been watching the game while glancing in my direction. "He just had the wind knocked out of him."

I breathed a sigh of relief. It would have been ridiculous to have my football career end on my first play.

Coach Payne put his hands on my shoulder pads and looked me in the eye. "All right, kid. Take ninety-nine's spot for this series. Those guys cleaned your clock—do something good to get even."

I pulled on my helmet, raced onto the field, and tapped ninety-nine on the shoulder. He frowned but then ran off.

On first down, Hunter handed off to our running back, who banged out a couple of yards. I put a block on the cornerback guarding me—nothing sensational, but my chip kept him out of the play.

In the huddle, Hunter looked at me. "You ready?"

I nodded.

"Okay. Left slant eighty-two on 'Rocket.'"

I lined up on the left, my feet set properly. On Hunter's 'Rocket,' I took three hard steps upfield and broke to the middle. It was a route we'd practiced over and over at Gilman Park in the summer. Hunter's pass was on target. I was about to reach out for the ball when from the corner of my eye I saw J'Varre bearing down on me. I pulled my arms in, letting the ball sail right by me.

J'Varre didn't pull off. His shoulder drove right into my stomach for the second time, again knocking me flat. I didn't see the interception, didn't see the guy run Hunter's pass back for a TD.

I struggled to my knees and jogged off the field. I found a spot at the end of the bench, yanked off my helmet, dry-retched a few times, and then puked up the yogurt, the blueberry muffin, and the Cheerios.

CHAPTER 5

I was back home a little before one. I found a hot-water bottle in the closet, filled it, and lay down on the sofa. I placed the hot-water bottle on my stomach, and the heat slowly went down into my body and took some of the pain away.

After about thirty minutes, I heard a key in the front door, and a second later my mother was standing over me.

"Your coach called," she said. "He told me you might have broken ribs." Her tone was more angry than concerned. "I called Doctor Jain, and he can see you at two."

"I'm fine, Mom. Nothing's broken."

"You're going to the doctor, Brock, and that's final."

Forty-five minutes later, a technician at Dr. Jain's x-rayed my ribs and then led me to an examining room. Minutes later, Dr. Jain came in. I lay down on a sheet of white butcher paper while he pushed down on my chest. "Does that hurt?"

"No."

He pushed again. "How about that?"

"A little."

"Take a deep breath. Pain?"

"Not much."

He poked a little more and then left to look at the x-rays. When he came back, he gave me a thumbs-up. "Nothing's broken. You'll feel better in a day or two."

On the drive home, my mother hardly talked. It was as if she was angry that I *didn't* have broken ribs. At dinner, my father asked me about the play. "It was a slant pass over the middle."

He frowned. "You've got to protect yourself on those. Your coach must have told you that."

"Obviously, telling wasn't good enough," my mother said, her voice clipped. She took her plate to the sink, putting it down so hard, it broke in half.

After dinner, I went to my room and closed my door. It didn't help—I could still hear my parents arguing in the living room. I couldn't make out what was said, but it went on and on.

The next morning, my mom came into the kitchen while I was eating breakfast and sat across from me. "I don't suppose I can talk you into quitting."

I didn't answer.

She sat looking at me for a long time. Finally, she

sighed, started to stand, and then sat down again. "Can I ask you a favor?"

"Sure."

"Join the chess club at Crown Hill High."

It was so out of left field that I wasn't sure I'd heard her right.

"The chess club?"

She nodded. "You know how to play, don't you?"

"Sort of. Dad taught me, but I haven't played since fifth grade. Why do you want me to join the chess club?"

"Because your dad loves chess. You could play against him. It'd be something you'd have in common. Whatever is driving this football thing will end, but you two could play chess your whole lives."

CHAPTER 4

Crown Hill High was built piecemeal, so one wing is one hundred years old, while the other wing looks brand new. The long, narrow hallway connecting the two wings is called Suicide Alley. If a junior or senior wants to harass a freshman, that's where it's most likely to happen.

I was weaving my way through Suicide Alley, heading to my first class, when I spotted Hunter Gates. He radiated power, like a hunk of uranium. He had a bunch of kids around him — football players, other athletes, and nice-looking girls.

I sort of mumbled "Hello," but he ignored me. I'd dropped his pass; I'd caused an interception; I was on the freshman team. Once he passed by, I breathed a sigh of relief. Okay — as far as he was concerned, I didn't exist. But better to be invisible than to be the next Jerry Jumper.

The classes at Crown Hill High weren't much

different from classes in middle school. History, P.E., math, English, general science, and Spanish. I had English fourth period with Ms. Ringleman. I arrived a few minutes before the bell and spotted an empty seat next to an Asian kid. Was he the kid at Gilman Park whose father had been yelling at his mother, the kid who'd been shoved around by those losers?

"Anybody sitting here?" I asked.

He turned toward me, and I knew it was him. Physically he was the anti-Hunter—the last guy in the world you'd call handsome. He had black hair that stuck up, big ears that stuck out, and a chubby face. He wasn't tall, but he looked strong in a fireplug way. "Eleven big-breasted girls have begged to sit there," he said, his voice and face deadly serious, "but I have saved the seat for you, my Caucasian friend."

I laughed a little—what else could I do?—and took the seat.

When Ms. Ringleman called roll, I learned his name was Richie Fang. Kids snickered as he said, "Here." Ms. Ringleman looked down to her class list to put a check next to his name.

As soon as her eyes were off him, Fang made a vampire face, sticking his front teeth out, forming his hands into claws, and then lurching toward me. Instinctively, I pulled back, and kids laughed again. Ms. Ringleman's head snapped up. Fang's face became the picture of innocence, making kids laugh more and making Ms. Ringleman tell us all to quiet down.

When class ended, I headed to the lunchroom to meet the McDermotts and Trevor Marino. As I made my way down the hallway, Richie Fang walked right by my side, jabbering away about the book *Ender's Game,* as if we were lifelong friends. I nodded a few times, unable to shake him. In the cafeteria, I spotted my friends. I got my food and then took a seat at their table. Richie Fang plopped down next to me. "I'm Richie Fong," he said.

That took me back. "I thought your name was Fang."

"No. It's spelled F-A-N-G but it's pronounced 'Fong.'"

Rory tilted his head, confused. "If it's pronounced 'Fong,' why don't you spell it F-O-N-G?"

"Because my parents are Chinese."

It made no sense, but Richie gave out a big laugh, so we laughed along.

He talked nonstop, telling his life story all through the lunch period. His family had moved to the Seattle area two years ago. He'd gone to Canyon Park Middle School in Bothell. Before that, he'd lived in San Francisco, and before that in China in a city that he sometimes called Nanking and sometimes Nanjing. His parents both worked for UW as research scientists. "They're world-renowned experts on genital herpes," he said, laughing loudly. Nobody other than Richie knew what genital herpes was, but we laughed too. Like me, he had no brothers or sisters, but he loved animals. "In my room in Nanjing, I had twenty-three cockatiels that flew around my room, pooping wherever they wanted, sometimes on my head."

That was too much. "Come on," I said. "You didn't own twenty-three cockatiels."

He stuck his hand out. "You want to bet me? All right. Bet me. Twenty bucks."

How could I prove he hadn't had twenty-three birds in China, or a hundred and twenty-three?

"I'm not betting," I answered.

Richie's face was stern. "So you admit I owned twenty-three cockatiels in Nanking."

I looked to Trevor for help, but he just shrugged.

"Whatever," I said.

Richie smiled, turned to Trevor, motioned back at me with his thumb, and whispered, "He thinks I let twenty-three cockatiels poop on my head!"

The whole thing was loony, and none of us really got the joke, but Richie laughed, so we laughed.

Once I'd finished eating, I looked around the cafeteria. In the morning announcements, I'd heard that there'd be a chance to sign up for clubs during lunch, and I remembered my promise to my mother.

I spotted a sign for the chess club in the west corner. I picked up my tray and stood. "I'll talk to you guys later. I'm going to sign up for the chess club."

"The chess club?" Tim said. "Since when do you play chess?"

I tried to sound sure of myself. "My dad taught me. It's a good game."

As I started off, Richie was again at my elbow. "I play chess too," he said as we first bused our dishes and then wound our way through the tables and chairs to the back corner. "My rating is eighteen thirty-seven. There's an Internet site—Red Hot Pawn. We can play every night. My screen name is Vampire17. Can you believe there are sixteen other chess-playing vampires?"

The guy was mildly entertaining, but I wasn't ready to sign on to be his best friend. "I'm pretty busy."

Fang's face grew serious. "Eighteen thirty-seven is a very good rating. I could help you."

Other clubs had long lines of kids waiting to sign up, but not the chess club. Mr. Gupta, the coach, beamed as he took our names. "My room will be open at lunch every day," he said, speaking with a clipped, singsong accent. "The more you play, the better you will get. We will participate in competitions throughout the year. You will never regret this. Other games are for a day; chess is for life."

After we signed up, Richie grabbed my forearm. "I have to talk to you. I have to explain."

Before I could object, he pulled me to a spot by a janitor's closet. His dark eyes bore into me. "You remember me from the summer. I know you do. You were playing soccer, and I was with my parents. And then those idiots came along."

"I sort of remember. You ate lunch, right?"

"My dad is not a bad man."

"Why would I think anything bad about your dad?" I protested. "I don't even know your dad."

"Because he was yelling, and my mom was crying. But it wasn't what it looked like."

"I didn't notice anything. You don't have to explain."

He ignored me, his words rushing out. "My mom has cancer. When she won't eat, my dad screams at her because he's afraid she's going to die."

Behind us, food trays clattered as they were dumped into busing bins. Voices shouted back and forth across the room. Some teacher was making an announcement with a bullhorn. "We are going to be friends," he said. "You and me, so you need to know."

The bell rang, and then we were both off to our next class.

CHAPTER

There were fifteen hundred students at Crown Hill High. Most kids walked the halls, laughing and joking with friends, just like I did, just like Richie did. How many of them had bad stuff going on at home? A parent who was sick or a drug addict or a drunk? Or just a house where everyone screamed all the time, or where they never saw their dad or their mom? How many kids had lives that had gone off the rails? It couldn't be only Richie and me.

That night, I went to Red Hot Pawn and signed up, giving myself the screen name of Renaldo2. I searched for Vampire17, and I sent out a challenge. I waited for a few minutes. Nothing. I was about to log on to Minecraft when a message appeared in the upper-right-hand corner of the screen: *Challenge accepted.*

I remembered enough about chess to start the game,

but within a few moves I was in deep trouble, and within twelve I knew checkmate was near. At the top of the screen was a little box that said *Message Opponent.*

I clicked on the box and typed, *I know how it is with your mom, because . . .* My fingers stopped. I deleted what I'd written and made my move.

Four moves later, he checkmated me with his queen. I wrote *Good game* in the message box and logged off.

The next morning, when I stepped inside Ms. Ringleman's classroom, Richie's eyes lit up as if we were lifelong friends. The seat next to him was empty, he pointed to it, and so I had to take it. After class, he chattered away at my elbow as I walked to the cafeteria. When the other guys saw him, they gave me a look.

Again?

I shrugged, and then suddenly I didn't care what they thought. They could go to another table, or I'd go to another table—I wasn't telling Richie Fang to get lost.

When I was with my Whitman friends, I knew what they were going to say before they said it, but I never knew what to expect from Richie. His mind was as fast as a hummingbird's wings. High school was supposed to be different, a place where you learned new stuff. Richie was different. And we had a bond, a sort of secret partnership, even if only I knew it.

What people think and say about Richie now, the way they judge him—they don't know the whole story, and they don't want to know it. They want heroes and villains, like in a cartoon. I'm not defending what Richie did, because he was wrong, but other wrongs came first.

Lots of them.

CHAPTER 6

Freshman football practice started after school that day. Everything about the team was slightly off. Our equipment was old; we practiced on a baseball field; the bathroom was five minutes away. We had only one coach and only four parent volunteers, and on the first day one of the parents didn't show up. I felt some relief—none of those huge older guys were around to annihilate me—but mainly I felt let down.

Coach Quist, a big guy with a beer belly, had us stretch, run wind sprints, hit the blocking dummies, stretch more, run obstacle courses, and hit the dummies more before he finally let wide receivers run pass routes. The quarterbacks, two guys whose names sounded the same—Aiden and Kaiden—took turns flinging the ball downfield to us. After catching Hunter's passes for weeks, working with Aiden and Kaiden was like trading in a Lamborghini for a junker.

Neither had the arm strength to get the ball down the field or to the sideline. I'd run an out pattern and break into the clear but then have to come back to try to make the catch. That gave the safety time to break up the pass.

There weren't enough bodies on the freshman team for anyone to play just one position, so Coach Quist stuck me on defense as the nickel back on passing downs. "Play off the receiver and then—once the ball is in the air—break on it. Think interception. Use that speed. Be a game changer."

He was upbeat, but the parent volunteers seemed bored. During water breaks, I'd look over at the field where varsity practiced. I couldn't see much, but I saw enough to know that Hunter wasn't clicking with his receivers—too many of his passes were bounding wildly downfield, and nobody was getting open on deep patterns.

That kept a spark of hope alive in me. Hunter needed to put up big numbers to keep college recruiters interested, which meant he'd need somebody to catch the deep ball. If nobody on the varsity could make the big catch, they'd have to look to the freshman team. Sure I'd screwed up the tryout, but Mr. Gates was still on the sidelines, and I was still the fastest receiver on either squad.

CHAPTER 7

I didn't see what happened to Richie at school the next Monday, but I heard about it. Everybody heard about it.

He was walking through Suicide Alley, being his normal self—talking loud, telling stupid jokes, laughing his high-pitched laugh. He must not have been looking where he was going, because he plowed into the one person in the school you don't want to plow into—Hunter Gates.

Bad enough, but instead of apologizing, Richie pointed his finger at Hunter and went into a Hollywood tough cowboy imitation. "This school ain't big enough for the two of us, pardner."

I can picture Richie saying it, picture the scowl on his face and hear the craziness in his voice. He meant no harm; he never meant harm. He was always ready to laugh, and he figured everyone else was too.

He was wrong.

Hunter grabbed Richie by his shirt collar and—lifting

him off the ground—walked him back to the double doors that led to the faculty parking lot. Hunter kicked the metal bar hard with his foot and the door flew open. Then he threw Richie out the door, like the muscle guys at a nightclub throw out gatecrashers. Richie fell backwards onto the lawn, his books and papers flying out of his backpack and onto the grass. Hunter pointed a finger at him. "You're right, China Boy. This school isn't big enough for both of us."

During warm-ups at football practice after school, guys on the team repeated the story, laughing as they told it. None of them knew Richie's name, so he was the Chinese kid with the big ears, or the Asian guy with the hair that stuck straight up. They talked about how white his face had gone, how his books and papers had flown everywhere, and how strong Hunter Gates was. "It was like the kid weighed one pound," Aiden said. "Hunter tossed him out the door like he was a Styrofoam cup."

The next day, I thought Richie might be hanging his head, or even hiding. If Hunter Gates had come after me, I'd have tried to disappear for a few weeks. But not Richie.

"Over here, quick," he called out as I stepped into Ms. Ringleman's room. "Three cheerleaders have been pestering me for your seat. They said, 'Oh, oh, Handsome Richie. If you let us sit next to you, you can make out with us all through class.' But I said, 'No, this desk is for my friend Brock.'" Kids around him laughed, and even Ms. Ringleman smiled.

After class, we headed to the cafeteria. That's when he finally did change. Hunter was sitting at a table in the middle of the cafeteria, surrounded by his pack of friends. Instead of sitting with the McDermotts and Trevor—who were a couple of tables from Hunter—Richie led me to a spot as far from Hunter as possible. I bought a cheeseburger and fries at the counter. When I returned, he motioned with his head toward Hunter. "Do you know him?"

"Hunter Gates? Everybody knows him. He's the quarterback of the football team. He was all-league as a freshman, but he was crappy last year. He was always mean, and having a bad season has made him meaner."

Richie's eyes dropped. "You heard about yesterday?"

"Yeah, I heard."

"He saw me in the hall today and called me Fang-Face. He told me if I said a word, he'd shove my violin up my butt. How does he know my name? And how does he know I play violin? I don't get why he hates me. I was just joking."

"Stay away from him, Richie. In a couple of weeks, he'll forget about you."

We both went silent. I ate my cheeseburger while Richie used chopsticks to eat a noodle dish he'd brought from home. "What do you say we go play chess in Mr.

Gupta's room," he said when we'd finished. "We've got fifteen minutes."

We slipped out a side door and headed to Mr. Gupta's room. Gupta had set out two long tables, one for beginners and the other for advanced players. Richie went to the advanced table and started a game with an Indian kid named Rohan who was in my P.E. class. As soon as the game got going, Richie went back to being Richie.

"What goes 'Ha ha . . . plop?'"he said in voice that filled the room. He waited a beat, then answered: "A guy laughing his head off."

Everybody groaned.

I looked over at the beginners' table and spotted Anya Lin, the girl from Whitman Middle School who'd come in second in the science competition. Anya had dark hair and dark eyes and a smile that made you want to smile back. She wasn't curvy like girls on hot Internet sites, but she wasn't skinny, either. The chair across from her was empty.

Her eyes brightened when she saw me, and she motioned for me to move to her table. That's how it was the first weeks of high school. Everybody was glad to see anyone they knew.

"I didn't know you played chess," she said as I sat down across from her.

"I'm basically a total beginner," I admitted.

"Me too. I'm only doing this because my dad says I'll

need extracurricular activities to get into a top college, and I suck at sports."

We started a game. My goal was to avoid an idiotic blunder and a humiliating loss. Anya was ahead by one knight as the lunch period neared an end. "How about we call it a draw?" she said, reaching her hand across the table.

"Draw it is," I said, giving her hand a shake.

She stood. "What's your next class?"

"General science. How about you?"

"AP Geometry."

The bell rang, and we were off—me to my regular classes, and Richie and Anya to advanced math, advanced science, advanced everything.

CHAPTER 8

When I got home that night, a big stationary bicycle was taking up half the den. My dad was sitting on it, his legs slowly—so slowly—moving up and down. He stopped pedaling as soon as he saw me, and he forced himself to smile. "What do you think of it?" he asked.

My mom came out from the kitchen. "Isn't it great?" she said, her voice too cheery.

The blood was pounding in my ears. It was so wrong, all of it, but I couldn't say it. "It looks like fun," I managed. "I might use it too."

My dad's smile disappeared. "No, Brock, you stay outside in the sunshine."

We ate dinner, and then I climbed upstairs to my room and logged on to the Internet. I searched "Steinert's disease and exercise." I found three articles, and all three said the same thing. Exercise wouldn't hurt, and there was a slight chance it could help. "If nothing else," one doctor wrote, "it gives the patient the feeling that he is fighting back."

The exercise bike wasn't the only change. When I got home after practice a couple of days later, my dad's car was gone and a new van was in front of the house in its place. The license plate had an icon of a wheelchair and the letters *DP* before the numbers. My dad was in the driver's seat, and a skinny red-haired guy was sitting in the passenger seat, his hand pointing to some control on the dashboard.

I waved to my dad, but he was so focused on whatever the redheaded guy was saying that he didn't see me. I went into the house.

"Is that Dad's?" I asked my mom, who was looking out the window at the van.

"Yes. And, Brock, it's a great thing. A tremendous thing. He can use his hands to brake, his thumb to accelerate."

I felt sick inside. "Does he really need that? I mean — "

My mother interrupted. "Brock, he needs it. Maybe not today, but soon. Because of that van, he'll be able to drive for years. But he's embarrassed about it, so don't ask him too many questions, okay?"

"I won't say anything," I mumbled.

She shook her head. "No, that's no good. You have to say something. Just be positive."

CHAPTER 9

The freshman team opened the season with an away game against Woodinville, a city at the northern end of Lake Washington. Both teams had first-game jitters. Guys jumped offside, made false starts, fumbled handoffs, and dropped passes. All the perfect-form tackles disappeared now that the sleds and the dummies were gone. A good tackle meant getting the guy down any way possible.

At halftime the game was scoreless, and it stayed scoreless through the third quarter. Whenever we made a big play, we were sure to follow it with a fumble or a penalty. Woodinville did no better. I ran good routes and got open, but Aiden didn't throw a single ball my way.

With about four minutes left, though, our running game suddenly clicked. Our running back, Blake Tuckett, sliced through the Woodinville line for gain after gain. We roared down the field, moving from our twenty-seven to their six-yard line. It looked like we'd score easily, but on third-and-goal from the two, one of our linemen jumped offside, changing it to third-and-seven.

Thirty seconds were left in the game. Coach Quist called time out and had us huddle around him. "Eighty-eight slant," he barked. Then he looked right at me. "Catch the ball, Brock."

The ref blew his whistle. I trotted onto the field, taking deep breaths. All I had to do was look the ball in, catch it, and get across the goal line, and we'd win.

"Hut! Hut!" Aiden screamed.

I drove forward three steps and made my break over the middle. I was wide open, but where was the ball? I could feel Woodinville's linebacker bearing down on me. Finally, Aiden released his pass, a wobbly spiral with no zip.

Still, I could have reached out, grabbed it, and fallen into the end zone. Instead, I pulled my arms in and dropped my shoulders, curling up like a scared bug. The Woodinville linebacker got a piece of me, and I went down, but not hard. Aiden's pass skipped off the turf.

I stood and trotted to the sideline, trying to act as if it had been just a normal incomplete pass. Once we reached our sideline, Aiden yanked off his helmet and glared at me. I moved away from him and looked onto the field. If our kicker, Eli Watts, made the field goal, we'd win the game, and my play would be forgotten.

A twenty-three-yard field goal shouldn't be a big deal, even on the freshman team. But what happened next was insane. The snap was low. The ball skipped past the holder and bounced crazily downfield. Eli raced after the ball and tried to pick it up but ended up kicking it farther downfield. A Woodinville player scooped it up, and then he was off. He wasn't the fastest guy in the world, but no one tracked him down. From the Woodinville side, I heard a mixture of laughter and cheering.

"You alligator-armed that pass," Aiden said, coming over to me, pointing his finger. "You didn't have the guts to reach out and catch it. This loss is on you."

"Your pass was late," I shot back. But on the bus ride back to school, nobody said a word to me.

"How did it go?" my dad asked as soon as I stepped in the door, his eyes bright with expectation.

"We lost seven to zero," I muttered.

"Did you make any catches?"

"A couple," I lied. "A curl and a slant."

Saturday night, the varsity lost to Woodinville 23–0. I didn't go to the game, but I read about it in the Sunday *Seattle Times*. There was a small article in the print newspaper, but all the statistics were posted online. Hunter had thrown three interceptions and had fumbled twice. Colton Sparks made three catches but for only twenty yards, and no other receiver had caught more than one. I'd had a horrible game, but knowing that the varsity was terrible made me feel better.

CHAPTER 10

After my drop against Woodinville, Coach Quist demoted me to the second team. That meant my role on offense was to be the deep threat on a team that didn't have a quarterback who could throw deep.

Because of my speed, I did get some playing time on defense. Whenever our opponent absolutely had to throw, I was in the backfield as a nickel defender. My assignment was to play in the center of the field and knock down any deep throws. Twice in three games I actually did that, chasing down looping passes and slapping them away. Both times, I got pats on the back from the coaches and the other guys on the team. It wasn't much, but it was better than nothing.

As bad as things were going, I still had a tiny bit of hope. At practice, Hunter was throwing the ball great—I could see that from the freshman field—but the timing with his receivers wasn't there. Colton was the best of the bunch, but he was strictly a short- or medium-pass guy. And since no other receiver had the speed to go deep, defenses were pinching in. Hunter needed a receiver who could stretch the field.

I hadn't actually seen any of the varsity games. Rory and Tim had been asking me to go with them, but I'd been turning them down. They'd started hanging out with guys who got drunk whenever they got hold of beer or wine, so I never knew whether they were truly going to the game. The last thing I needed was to get caught doing something stupid. I couldn't ask Richie—he wouldn't want to sit in the cold and cheer for Hunter Gates. As for asking Anya—I didn't have the nerve. So I followed Hunter's season on the Internet, pulling up the stats for every game and poring over them.

His numbers sucked. He was near the bottom of the league in completion percentage, yardage, and touchdown passes. The only thing he led the league in was interceptions.

After the varsity had lost their fourth straight game, I went to Recruits.com to see where he stood. I scanned the list once, then a second time, then a third. One hundred quarterbacks were listed, but Hunter wasn't one of them.

CHAPTER 11

At the beginning of September, nobody at Crown Hill High knew Richie Fang. Six weeks later, everyone knew him. Every other day, Mr. Spady, the principal, said his name at the top of the morning announcements. Richie took second place in a statewide math contest, first in an architectural design contest, first in a UW violin competition. The guy was a trophy factory.

Some kids congratulated him, bumping knuckles and high-fiving him in the hall. Most kids ignored him. But not Hunter, and not anybody in Hunter's crowd. The more times Richie's name came over the intercom, the more they ridiculed him, calling him Fang-Face and Fungus and Fing-a-ling and worse.

Most of the stuff that happened to Richie was invisible to me. But sometimes after Ms. Ringleman's class, I'd be with him as Hunter and his posse came at us from the opposite direction. Usually Hunter would walk straight at Richie, forcing him to step to the left or right. Whichever way Richie chose, Hunter would go that way too, not letting Richie get by. Finally, Richie would turn sideways, his back pressed against the wall, a lock digging into his spine. Hunter would grin and say, "See you later, Fang."

And then there was the Twitter post. Somebody took a picture of Richie naked in the locker room one afternoon and then posted it that night on an account called @FangsLittleWang. I never saw it, but I heard about it. Everybody heard about it.

When kids spotted Richie in the halls the next morning, they snickered. For a while, Richie didn't know what was going on, but he soon found out. By noon, somebody had told Mr. Spady, and by the end of the school day, Twitter had taken down the post.

The next morning, every homeroom teacher talked about cyberbullying and how it was a crime, and that if anybody knew anything, they should come forward. The teachers were trying to do the right thing, I guess, but all those lectures did was to make it certain that everybody in the school knew about @FangsLittleWang.

I wanted to say *Don't let it bother you* to Richie, but that would be so weak. The entire school is saying that you've got a little wang, and you're not supposed to let it bother you?

"In one week, nobody will remember any of this," I said.

He snorted. "Right. And in two weeks, Hunter Gates will knit me some nice warm mittens for the winter."

CHAPTER 12

The football season dragged on. Hunter's stats picked up when he threw a couple of touchdown passes and the varsity team actually won a game, but the next week he threw two interceptions in a loss.

The freshman team wasn't doing any better, and I was doing nothing at all. In two games, I'd been on the field for only four offensive plays, and I hadn't had a single pass thrown in my direction. Coach Quist used me as a nickel back a little more often, but not much.

After each game, my dad asked me a couple of questions, and I told some version of the same old lies. "I caught a couple of balls, and I made a tackle on special teams. We're mainly a running team, though." He'd smile and say something like "The main thing is to get out there and compete." And that would be that for a week.

My mom had stopped pestering me about concussions or injuries. For a time, that surprised me, but then

I figured it out. She washed my uniform after every game—and most of the time it really didn't need washing. She knew how little playing time I was seeing.

Halloween came and went, and then there were just two games left in the season. The first was on a Friday, right after school, against Roosevelt on our home field. For three quarters, it was just like every other game. Fumbles, penalties, the occasional long run, a botched play. It was actually worse than most games for me, because I hadn't been involved in a single play on offense or on defense.

With a little more than a minute left in the fourth quarter, we were losing 10–6. I was sitting at the end of the bench holding my helmet in my hand and fighting down a yawn, wishing the season were over.

We had the ball—fourth-and-one—on our own forty-yard line. Aiden was up over center when suddenly Coach Quist screamed, "Time out! Time out!" A whistle blew, and Coach turned to me.

"Get your helmet on, Brock. You're in for the next play."

I sat, frozen.

"You heard me. Now move!"

I jumped up, pulled the helmet on, snapped the chin strap, and joined the huddle around Coach Quist. "Okay," he said, leaning forward. "We're going to go power formation with Brock split right. Aiden, you fake the handoff and then throw that ball as far as you can down the center of the field. Just heave it." Quist stopped, then looked at me. "Got that?" I nodded. "All right, then. On three."

We ran back onto the field and took our spots on the line. I was split ten yards to the right. A cornerback was on me, but the safety was way up, anticipating a running play.

Aiden looked over the line and then shouted, "Hut! Hut! Hut!"

I took off. Aiden faked a handoff, dropped back three steps, and then flung the ball. The Roosevelt safety had bitten on the fake, and I'd blown by the cornerback guarding me. I looked up and found the ball, but instead of being out in front where I could run to it, it was behind me. I had to twist my body and reach back. I felt the ball hit my hands. I bobbled it once . . . twice . . . and then had it in my fingertips. I regained my balance, pulled the ball tight to my chest, looked up, and saw nothing but green grass in front of me. I ran and ran and ran, until I was in the end zone, and then I ran until I was through the end zone, and only then did I turn around.

My teammates were racing toward me, huge grins on their faces. I'd done it! It had come out of nowhere, but I'd done it. I'd gone sixty yards for a touchdown in the last minute of the Roosevelt game. A hoard of guys surrounded me. Aiden pounded my back so hard, it hurt. The whistle was blowing, so we all raced to the sideline before we got an unsportsmanlike-conduct penalty.

Coach Quist was waiting for me. He slapped my helmet and shook me by my shoulders. "Great play! Great play!"

We missed the extra point—we didn't make a single kick all year, and the varsity kicker made only a couple—but we won 12–10. That night at dinner, I described the play to my dad. When I was finished, he fired question after question at me, his eyes and face lit up for the first time in a long time. Seeing him smile made my mom smile.

CHAPTER 13

The next day, I was a minor celebrity at school. My friends from Whitman — the McDermotts and those guys — congratulated me, and so did Richie and Anya, though I don't know how they found out about my touchdown.

As I suited up for practice, guys on the team patted me on the back again. On the practice field, Coach Quist talked about the victory, but he didn't mention my name. Then he told us it was time to turn our attention to the next game. "It's our last game of the year," he said. "Put it all out there." My glory time was over.

Thirty minutes into practice, I spotted Mr. Gates walking toward our field. I'd seen him at all the varsity practices, working with Hunter on technique. There were four or five other fathers like him — volunteer coaches — but they came fewer times once the losses mounted. Hunter's dad was the only regular.

As he strode toward Coach Quist, he looked in my direction and waved. Was he waving to me? I turned around. No one. I gave him a small wave back.

I was doing stretching exercises when Coach Quist called me over. I hustled to where he stood—shoulder to shoulder—with Mr. Gates. "Get your gear, Brock," Coach Quist said when I reached them. "You're playing on the varsity this week."

My mouth dropped open.

"Me?"

Coach Quist nodded, not looking happy. "Yeah, you. So gather your stuff. Mr. Gates will explain."

My "stuff" was a water bottle. I grabbed it and walked with Mr. Gates. As we moved off, the guys on the freshman team watched. Once they learned I'd been promoted, they'd be angry. They'd busted their butts game after game, while I'd been on the bench for ninety-five percent of the plays. I'd made *one* good play all year. One.

Walking fast, Mr. Gates explained the plan. "Coach Payne heard about your TD catch. I told him that you and Hunter had worked together in the summer and that you had good hands and great speed. You'll play only a handful of downs against Bothell High. You'll be split out wide, almost out-of-bounds—a good five yards farther out than the normal spot for a wide receiver. You won't block anybody, and we won't expect you to take any kind of hit. Bothell knows Hunter hasn't connected on any long passes all year. They might rotate a safety over the first few times we use this formation, but if we don't throw to you in the first half, in the second half, you'll only get one-on-one coverage. When they least expect it, you run a fly pattern; Hunter throws a strike. Bang! We score." He paused. "At least, that's the plan."

I swallowed. "Sounds great."

He put his hand on my elbow and squeezed tight. "Listen to me, kid. This year has been a nightmare for Hunter. Everybody who sees him play knows he has talent. But the mental part—it's getting to him. He needs something positive to take into the off-season, something to build on for next year. You could be that first brick."

It was a strange week of practice. The varsity guys were beat up by the long season, so Coach Payne went easy on them. After the warm-ups, he had them run through the plays, but with absolutely no hitting. Most of the time I stood off by myself, watching. Nobody on the varsity knew me, but I knew what they thought. I was the guy who had good hands and could run like lightning, but who also had a yellow streak down his back.

Every so often, we'd practice my play. I'd line up close to the sideline and run out, at about eighty percent speed, making it easy for the cornerback to cover me. But once or twice every practice, when Coach Payne turned his clipboard upside down, I'd turn on the jets and run a fly pattern. Usually the play didn't work. The safety would be back, or Hunter wouldn't have enough time to make a good pass. Of the ten times he threw long that week, I caught two.

On Thursday during lunch, Richie asked me what my parents thought about my promotion to varsity. "I haven't told them," I replied.

"Why not?"

"I'm probably going to be in four plays all game and do nothing. My mom is so afraid I'll get killed that she won't watch football, and I don't want my dad to drive all the way out to Bothell just to see me run downfield a few times. We have no chance of winning."

For a while, Richie didn't answer. "Did you ever see *The Music Man*?" he finally asked.

"Never even heard of it."

"It's a movie. Well, it was a play first. A musical. It's really good, especially the opening. Anyway, at the end all these grade school kids march around playing their band instruments. They totally suck, but their parents clap like maniacs. Your dad will be like that. Seeing you on the field in a varsity uniform will make him proud." He paused. "Your dad's got something wrong with him, doesn't he?"

The blood rushed out of my head. How did Richie know?

"I saw him with your mom a while ago," Richie said. "At the Bartell Drugs on Fifteenth. He was using those arm-brace things to help him walk, and your mom was right by his side."

I could picture my dad moving slowly up the aisles, my mom helping him. How Richie knew they were my parents was a mystery, but what did it matter? He knew.

"He's got a muscular disease," I said,

"Can they fix him?"

I shook my head. "Not now, but they're working on it. Researchers are always coming up with new cures. Pretty soon they'll have something."

Richie nodded. "That's good, that's good. It's the same with my mom. The doctors got most of the cancer with surgery and chemo the first time, but she might need more chemo to get the last bit."

We both fell silent, and then he put his fist toward me. I gave him a bump, and a smile. "Let's go to Gupta's room. I want to beat that Rohan kid, and I know you want to lose yourself in Anya's dreamy dark eyes."

When I told my dad I'd been promoted to varsity, he was surprised. "Now? For the last game?"

"It's because of my touchdown catch. Coach Payne put in a new play just for me. He's got me split way out, and I run a straight fly pattern or a deep post. They'll use it only once or twice all game. Either I'll make a big play or I'll do nothing."

He considered for a moment. "That's smart. It uses

your speed and puts you in a place to succeed. When's the game?"

"I'll be on the field only for a couple of snaps. It doesn't make sense for you to go."

"What are you talking about? Of course I'll be there. I bet you Mom will go too. She's not as nervous about football as she used to be."

CHAPTER 14

The game was Saturday night in Bothell. Saturday came up cold and wet. Some juniors and seniors might drive fifteen miles to watch a lousy team try to finish the season with a win, but my friends were freshman; none of them would be there.

Bothell had clinched a spot in the playoffs the previous week. For them, the game was a tune-up for a state title run. All they wanted to do was avoid injuries.

After I changed into my uniform, my mom drove me to the school parking lot, where the team bus was waiting. The bus ride was brutal. Diesel fumes filtered into the bus, and on Bothell Way the bus hit one red light after another. My stomach churned from both nerves and the ride, but I was determined not to barf a second time in front of the varsity guys.

Once the bus reached the stadium, we stored our stuff

in the visitors' locker room before taking the field. There had never been more than one hundred people at any of my freshman games, but the entire city of Bothell was in the stands. The Cougar marching band played the theme song from *Rocky* as the Bothell High team raced onto the field with fireworks exploding behind them.

After our warm-ups, Hunter started throwing to me and the other receivers. As I went through the drills, crazy fantasies filled my head. I wouldn't be on the field for one play; I'd be on for many plays. I'd run fast and make leaping catches and score touchdowns. My name would be in the headline of the prep page of the *Seattle Times*.

Then the horn sounded—game time—and I jogged toward our bench. I was still sky-high with what I would do. That's when I spotted my dad walking next to my mom, about ten rows up from the field. His face was pale, his shoulders bent, his eyes fixed on the ground in front of him as he moved his braces forward. He'd always been the one to look out for anyone who was old or weak or sick. Now people were clearing space for him. I turned away.

I felt a hand on my shoulder—it was Coach Payne. "Listen up. If you do catch a ball today, and you see somebody closing on you, just fall down. Understand? Just drop like you've been shot."

"I can get some yards after the catch, Coach," I said. "I'm not afraid."

"Nobody's saying you're afraid. But this is your first varsity game, so we're going to keep things simple. Open space in front of you—run like hell. Tackler coming at you—drop, cover, and hold."

CHAPTER 13

The Bothell guys were fast and strong, but their heads weren't in the game. Why should they take us seriously? We were a crappy team finishing out a failed season. Win or lose, they were in the playoffs.

We caught an early break. Midway through the opening quarter, their center snapped the ball before the quarterback was ready. It soared over the QB's head and bounced around in their end zone until one of their guys fell on it. Still, it was a safety for us, putting us ahead 2–0.

Throughout the first half, Bothell kept doing dumb things—fumbles, holding penalties, botched hand-offs—to stop themselves. Probably they had a bunch of second-teamers out there—I don't know for sure.

When we had the ball, Coach Payne had Hunter running draws and option sweeps, eating up the clock. Every once in a while, Hunter would throw a quick slant over the middle to Colton or Ty Erdman, the slot receiver, but nothing went deep.

In the first half, Hunter drove the team into the red zone three times, but without a decent field-goal kicker, each time we had to go for it on fourth down. All three times, Hunter was stopped short. He was piling up yardage with his arm and his legs, but at halftime the score was still 2–0.

I'd been on the field twice, split wide. Both times, Coach Payne told me to run at about three-quarters speed. "Let them think you're nothing." I did what he said, all the time picturing my dad freezing up in the stands, his muscles growing stiff.

On the first drive of the second half, Bothell's offense took the kickoff and marched down the field, mixing up passes and runs, going seventy yards in seven plays for a touchdown. They were the hot knives, and our defense was the butter. Were these the first-string players? When the extra point split the uprights Bothell led 7–2, which sounded like a baseball score.

Throughout the third quarter, we stayed on the ground, making a few first downs and taking time off the clock before punting the ball away. The only passes Hunter threw were short completions to Colton or Ty. I took the field for a couple more plays, both times as a decoy.

When I entered the game early in the fourth quarter, the safety didn't even look over at me. When the ball was snapped, the cornerback didn't jam me or force me out of bounds. His eyes were peeking into the backfield; he was ready to leave me and give run support.

My heart pounded. Coach Payne had to see what had happened. The trap was set; he had lulled Bothell's defense to sleep. I could race by both defenders, get open deep, and catch a TD pass that would put us ahead. Fly eighty-eight was my play, and every time I stepped onto the field in the fourth quarter I expected Coach Payne to call it.

But he didn't.

And the clock kept ticking.

With four minutes left, the score was still Bothell 7, Crown Hill 2. Bothell had the ball on the fifty-yard line—fourth-and-two. They could punt the ball away, but if they made two more first downs, they'd be able to run out the clock and win the game. Their coach didn't hesitate; the Bothell offense stayed on the field. Bothell's fans roared approval.

They went on a quick count. The Bothell quarterback faked a handoff to his fullback and then rolled to his right. The tight end rolled with him and was wide open. Simple pass, simple catch, first down. But just as the QB released the ball, the tight end stumbled. He recovered, reached his hand up, and got his fingertips on the ball, but he couldn't haul it in. The ball flopped to the ground like a wounded duck.

We had one final chance, and we had good field position.

I paced the sidelines, praying to get into the game. On first down, Hunter gained four yards on a read-option play. On second, he was stopped for no gain, but on third down he completed a slant pass for five more yards, setting up a fourth-and-inches. That's when Coach Payne pushed me onto the field. "Now. Fly eighty-eight," he said. "Make the catch, kid."

I raced into the huddle. "Fly eighty-eight," I screamed at Hunter over the crowd noise. His eyes widened, and then they went ice cold. "You heard him," he said to the other guys. "On three."

Bothell, expecting a power run right up the middle, brought their linebackers and safeties close to the line of scrimmage. Our guys pinched in, making it seem like we were definitely pounding the ball up the middle. I split way outside, trying my best to look like a spectator.

The Bothell fans were on their feet, roaring; all eyes were on our running backs. Hunter took his position in the shotgun. "Rocket . . . Rocket . . . Rocket!" he screamed.

The center snapped the ball. As Hunter faked a handoff to the tailback, I blew by the cornerback guarding me, turning on the jets for the first time in the game. Bothell's safety never glanced my way.

I looked up, and there was the ball—high and soft—way out in front. A perfectly thrown ball.

Watch it in! Watch it in! Watch it in!

I ran, adjusting my angle just a little, reached out, and then had the ball in my hands. I clutched it to my chest as if it were a newborn baby that I was rescuing from a burning building. Green grass was in front of me, nothing but beautiful green artificial grass.

Once I crossed the goal line, I ran a few more yards and then turned around. The Bothell crowd was stunned into silence, but my teammates were charging me, all of them. Arms raised high and with huge grins and wide eyes. I looked from them toward the stands, but I couldn't find my dad or my mom.

We failed on the two-point conversion attempt, and Bothell got the ball back with one minute to play. I watched from the sidelines, afraid that they would make a miraculous play and steal the game back. But they were completely out of sync. An offside penalty, a dropped pass, a ball in the dirt, and then—on fourth down—a long prayer that wasn't answered.

We'd won.

On the bus ride back to Crown Hill High, guys came over to congratulate me on my catch. "I didn't want to go out a loser," Nate Nixon—a huge lineman—told me. Then he walloped me on the back so hard that a bolt of pain shot up my spine to my brain. Hunter was the last guy to come by.

"Nice catch."

CHAPTER 16

The lead article in the prep section of the Sunday *Seattle Times* described our upset of Bothell. It was mainly about Hunter—how he'd led our team with running and passing, how he'd finally shown signs of being the quarterback everyone had expected, how the next year would be his last chance to make a name and get a scholarship. My name wasn't in the article. "You made the catch," my dad said. "You scored the winning touchdown. You don't need the newspaper to tell you that."

In Monday's morning announcements, Mr. Spady gave the score and a cheer went up in classrooms. After that came an announcement about Richie. He'd made it to the finals of a violin competition that I hadn't known he was in. Spady slipped and pronounced his name "Fang," and people around me smirked.

All day, kids congratulated me, and I let the praise wash over me. But when the school day ended, I felt lost.

What was I supposed to do? For the first time since mid-August, my afternoon was empty.

I stood at the top of the stairs to the main entrance of the school looking toward downtown. The sky was dark gray, and a black cloud hung over Queen Anne Hill. I zipped up my jacket and was about to get going when I heard Richie's voice from behind. "Hold on. I'll walk with you."

We could feel the wind rising and a few warning raindrops. As we hurried home, he told me he'd heard about my catch, and I told him that it was great he'd made the violin finals. When we reached his house, I said goodbye and was about to continue home when he asked me if I wanted to see his project.

"What project?"

"The model of Crown Hill High. You know, for the ecological design contest in Portland. I told you about it a while ago."

"Right, right," I said, trying to remember. "Yeah, show me. I really want to see it."

He led me to the shed behind his house, opened the door, and switched on the light. On a sheet of plywood the size of a Ping-Pong table was a miniature Crown Hill High, only a transformed Crown Hill High—what Crown Hill High could become. A creek wound through the center of campus; an amphitheater took the place of the main parking lot. The cafeteria had a clear roof and an open-air eating area where the dumpsters now sat. The roofs of some of the buildings were covered in grass and moss; the roofs of others were covered with tiny solar panels. "This is *amazing,*" I said, leaning forward to get an even closer look.

He shrugged. "It's not done. I haven't started the main wing or the gym. And that glass roof looks great, but nothing is holding it up. The judges will notice that. Once I get the buildings finished, there's the detail work—painting the trees and bushes, putting in paths across the grass and bridges across the creek, adding streetlights. I haven't started on the athletic fields either. They'll go there."

I walked around the model. He was right—there was a lot left to do. "When is the contest?"

"The Portland contest is in June. If I win, the finals are in Pittsburgh in December."

"I could help if you want."

Immediately, I was afraid I was sticking my nose in where I wasn't wanted, but his face broke into a smile. "Would you really?"

For the next half hour, we measured green felt and laid it out on the back corner of the board, slowly creating a miniature baseball diamond. By the time we quit, the rainstorm had ended and my back hurt.

"Does that creek really exist?" I asked, pointing to a ribbon of blue that wound through the campus.

He nodded. "Yeah. People don't know it, but there are

a bunch of creeks that run to Puget Sound that are covered by roads. If you ask me, they should all be daylighted."

Suddenly, the shed door opened and Richie's mother stepped inside. When she saw me, she stepped back and covered her mouth, a little surprised sound leaking out.

I could hear the tension in Richie's voice as he introduced me. His mother made a small bow of the head, so I made a small bow back. Then she held out a plate. On it were a few little globs that looked like eyeballs from some sea creature. "I made you something," she said, speaking to Richie. "You share with your friend. I'll leave now." Then she said something in Chinese, and he answered in Chinese.

Once the shed door closed and we were alone, Richie held out the plate with the weird stuff on it. "They're called sago," he said, popping one into his mouth.

I picked one up, stuck the whole thing in my mouth, chewed a little, and swallowed. I thought it would be disgusting, but it didn't taste like much of anything. Maybe a little mango flavor, but just a little.

"It's good," I said.

After that, a quiet settled over us. He was leaning against his model; I sat down on the wheel of a lawnmower.

"Do you like to look at girls?" he asked, out of the blue.

"Sure," I said, surprised by the question. "Doesn't every guy?"

"I mean at their breasts."

"Yeah, of course," I said, confused. It was a question one of the McDermotts might have asked, but it was odd coming from Richie.

Richie frowned. "Breast cancer is making my mom sick, but I still like to look at girls' breasts. I look all the time."

I shrugged. "You and every other guy."

He picked another sago from the plate and popped it in his mouth, and then I ate the last one. "The first one weirded me out a little," I admitted as I chewed, "but these are pretty good."

I looked around for something new to talk about, and I spotted a couple of soccer balls in a box in the corner. I nodded toward them. "Do you play?"

He switched back to Richie the comedian. Even his voice changed. "Do I play? I am the greatest soccer player in the history of Canyon Park Middle School. Last year, I scored seventeen goals."

"Come on, be serious. Do you play?"

"I am serious. I'm a soccer stud. I can kick the ball long and far and straight, or I can bend it like Beckham." Then he grinned. "Would I make something up?"

CHAPTER 17

The touchdown catch made school better for me. Hunter and the other juniors and seniors nodded to me in the hallway, pointed a finger at me across a lawn. I was somebody.

I shouldn't have cared, considering the way Hunter was treating Richie. And if I'd dropped that pass and we'd lost the game, he would have looked for a chance to shove me into a garbage can and roll me down the back steps of the school—something that happened to at least one guy every year. But I *had* caught the pass; we *had* won the game. And that made me part of Hunter's circle. I was way out on the edge like Pluto. But I was in his orbit.

Most days when school ended, I'd walk with Richie to his home and we'd work on his eco-school. His mom would bring us some strange sugary thing that I'd end up liking.

I enjoyed working with Richie, letting time pass without thinking. But eventually I'd have to go home.

And when—ten minutes later—I stepped inside my own front door, I'd see my dad in the den doing his exercises, trying to keep up his strength.

And all that time, Christmas kept getting closer.

I'd always looked forward to Christmas; it was even better than my birthday. Every year, we drove to San Francisco, where my grandparents and my aunt Gina lived. Some years, my grandparents from my mom's side would be there too, though they stayed at a hotel and I didn't know them as well. During the day, I'd hang out with my cousins Mariah and Aaron. They'd take me to places like Fisherman's Wharf and Chinatown.

But this year, with my father the way he was, Christmas would be different. He couldn't drive all that way, which meant my mom would have to, and she hated to drive, especially over the snowy mountain passes. And once we reached San Francisco, I'd have to see my aunt and my grandparents looking at my dad. They knew what he had—I'd heard my mom tell them on the phone. They'd smile and pretend everything was fine, but nothing was fine. Probably I'd hear my mom whispering with them when my dad was in another room. I was sure my grandmother would cry, which would make my mom cry. And what would my cousins say to me? What would I say to them? I didn't want sympathy. I didn't want to explain.

I kept waiting for my dad or mom to say something about the trip to California, but by the time school let out on the twentieth and Anya asked me if I was going anywhere, no one had mentioned California yet. "I think I'm going to San Francisco," I told her.

"What do you mean? Don't you know?"

"Not really."

She looked at me as if I were crazy.

That night after dinner, I asked my mom.

"Would it disappoint you too much if we stayed home this Christmas?" she said. Her voice was quiet, but her neck turned bright red, which always happens to her when she gets nervous.

"No," I said, my voice steady. "It'd be fine with me."

"I know you like seeing everybody. We all do. But it's a long drive, and flying this time of year is expensive."

"Really, it's okay. I can help Richie with his project. His family lives in Nanjing, so he's not going anywhere."

Everything felt wrong Christmas Day. I got great gifts—some video games, clothes, an iTunes gift card—but there wasn't enough noise or people. The phone calls from San Francisco only made it worse.

CHAPTER 18

The second semester began mid-January. Just before Christmas break, I'd gone to the counselor and switched my P.E. class from volleyball to weight training. I had to get stronger.

When I walked into the weight room for the first time, almost the entire varsity football team was in the room, including Hunter. Football coaches always want guys to lift weights, so why not do it during school for credit instead of after school for nothing?

The teacher, Mr. Drager, passed out a list of suggested exercises, a warning sheet on steroid abuse, and a notebook for us to keep track of our progress. "I'll come around and help you with technique."

The varsity guys took over the back wall of the weight room, which had all the free weights on racks in front of huge mirrors. Some of the linemen were gigantic to begin with. If they got much bigger, they'd fill the room. I found myself a spot with other freshman and a few sophomores. As we worked out, we kept our eyes down and our voices low.

My leg strength was okay—you can't be quick with weak legs—but I had nothing in the way of upper body strength. The other freshmen around me—Trent Haslem, Cory Morris, J. J. Jones—bench-pressed at least thirty pounds more than I did.

Halfway through class, Hunter walked over to our side of the gym. "Hey, Ripley," he said, "I've got something for you." As he spoke, he tossed me handgrips. "Squeeze those every day. The stronger your hands, the more touchdown passes you'll catch."

I nodded, my head going up and down way too fast. "Sure, Hunter." He turned and walked back to his friends. The other freshmen stared at me, impressed.

On a Friday night a couple of weeks into the new semester, I got a text from Anya: *Call me when you can.* I immediately went to my contacts and hit the green button. The phone rang twice before she picked up. "What's up?" I said, trying to sound calm, hoping that she wanted to do something, anything, with me.

And she did.

Her second-semester elective was a class on the environment taught by Mr. Symonds. I didn't have Symonds, but everybody said he was funny—and smart and inspiring. He'd been arrested a couple of times during protests over police shootings of black men. He was huge on political activism, and Anya was huge on pleasing Mr. Symonds. "I want to make a difference in this world. What's the point of being alive if you don't?"

It was the coal train—Mr. Gates's coal train—that she'd picked out. She was planning to set up an informational table in the school cafeteria, and she wanted me to help her pass out leaflets and answer questions. "We'll do it every Friday, or at least every other Friday. The big energy companies are raping the environment. We've got to stop them."

As she talked, all I could see was Hunter. What would he do if he saw me handing out leaflets attacking his father's company?

"Can you pass out political stuff at school?" I asked when she stopped. "I mean, is it legal?"

"This is America, Brock. People can stand up and speak their minds."

"I know, Anya, but it's school, too, and we're aren't adults, so— "

"Are you going to help me or not?"

My hand was sweating so much, I had to switch the phone to my other ear. "Anya, I don't really know anything about the coal train, so— "

She interrupted. "It's Hunter Gates isn't it? His dad is the lawyer for the coal company. He's a big part of the problem, but you don't want to make Hunter mad at you. You're afraid of him."

"That's not fair, Anya. I'm not in Symonds's class. You know all about the coal trains, but I don't."

"Well, it would take about ten minutes of research to figure out that they're no good."

"You say that, but there's got to be another side. People like— "

"It's okay, Brock," she said, interrupting again. "I'll get somebody else."

CHAPTER 19

She got Richie.

Friday, the two of them sat behind a large table in the back of the cafeteria. Richie had built a diorama of the coal train to get people's attention. It wasn't anything like the model he was building of his eco-school, but it was effective. A miniature train—the cars filled with pepper to represent coal—was halfway across a map of Washington. Behind the train, the land was black; little plastic deer and coyotes were tipped onto their sides to show that everything was dead. The land in front of the train, including the Cascades, Puget Sound, and the Olympics, was still green. Above the diorama was a sign with letters in fiery red: BAN THE DEATH TRAINS!

Lots of kids stopped at the table. Anya and Richie handed them leaflets and answered questions about spills in Puget Sound and train explosions in Quebec and

Illinois and West Virginia and North Dakota. Just before the lunch period ended, I spotted Hunter on the other side of the cafeteria, glaring.

I didn't want oil and coal trains coming through Puget Sound, but I couldn't blame Hunter for being angry. People hate banks, and my dad works for one. If somebody were passing out leaflets saying that his bank was raping the environment and killing animals and people, I'd glare too. But that's all I'd do.

Hunter Gates would do more.

He didn't wait long. A week later, the morning announcements included the news that Richie would be playing a solo during a performance of the University of Washington Symphony Orchestra. I saw him before second period. "Way to go!" I said, giving him a knuckle bump.

Richie played an invisible violin for me and then bowed to an invisible audience. "I'm the man, Brock."

I gave him another knuckle bump and headed off just as a bunch of mainly Asian kids, maybe from his orchestra class or his math class, came up to him. Richie stood in the center of them, smiling, while they patted him on the back and shoved him this way and that.

I'd walked about twenty feet when I heard the voice. "Hey, Fang, I've got a question for you." I looked back.

Hunter.

Standing with him were Colton and other friends.

The hallway had gone quiet the way it does when everyone can feel that something bad is about to happen. The kids surrounding Richie had backed away.

"My name is pronounced 'Fong,'" Richie said, his voice loud and clear.

Hunter smiled mockingly. "Oh, it's *Fong*. So sorry, *Fong*. Now can I ask my question?"

"Ask whatever you want," Richie said.

"Are you gay?"

Richie's face went red. "What?"

"He asked if you were gay," Colton said. "So, are you?"

"No, I'm not gay," Richie shot back.

Hunter tilted his head. "I don't know if I can believe you, Fang. I mean, being a violin player seems pretty gay to me." He paused. "Do you kiss boys, Fang?"

There were at least twenty kids watching. A few of them laughed—a nervous, unhappy laugh—but most stayed silent, waiting. You could feel the violence in the air. Somebody needed to stop Hunter. Somebody needed to have the courage to step forward and tell him to shut his fat mouth. I wanted to be that somebody. I wanted to move forward, but my legs stayed rooted.

"No, I don't kiss boys," Richie said, his voice shaky.

Hunter, nine inches taller and seventy pounds heavier, took a step toward Richie. "But you'd like to, wouldn't you, Fang? I mean, if you could? Sloppy-wet

French kisses. Your tongue deep in some guy's mouth. You'd like that. I know you would. You'd like to do even more."

That did it. Richie dropped his backpack and charged Hunter, who turned aside quickly and—using Richie's momentum against him—gave Richie a shove that sent him toppling to the ground. He landed hard and then skidded forward on his belly, awkward and ugly. Hunter and Colton and the others looked at him for a second and hooted, and then they were gone, down the hall, turning once in a while to look back and laugh.

Richie pulled himself to his knees, then to his feet. Some kids helped him pick up the books and papers that had fallen out of his backpack. I took a step forward to help too, but a dozen kids were in front of me. I turned away and headed to class, my head down.

PART THREE

CHAPTER

Seattle schools get a week off in February around Presidents' Day. As soon as we returned from the break, Mr. Jacklin, the Crown Hill soccer coach, plastered flyers announcing soccer tryouts around the school.

If you'd asked me in December, I'd have said I wasn't going to turn out for soccer. But once I saw those flyers, I felt the itch. I'd played on a soccer team every year since turning six years old. Most of the Whitman guys would be trying out. And I wanted something to do after school, instead of going home early and seeing my dad sitting in his chair.

Richie had said he played soccer, and I seventy percent believed him, though I doubted he could bend it like Beckham. As I sat down in Ms. Ringleman's class, I dropped the flyer onto Richie's desk. "Did you see this?"

It's hard to describe how he'd changed after the whole "gay" thing in the hallway. Nothing more had happened between him and Hunter, or at least nothing that I heard about. Richie joked a little before class; he joked more at chess club. But I never saw him in the main hallways, so he must have been using side hallways to go from class to class. As soon as school ended, he was off campus, heading home, one of the first guys out the door. He never waited for me.

"Yeah, I saw it," he said.

"Are you turning out?"

Some of the old Richie came back. "I told you—I'm the best."

"So you really do play soccer."

"Soccer is my game, Brock. It's my only game, but it's my game. I'm good." His eyes got the crazy-funny look that I used to see all the time. He turned his face sideways, stuck his teeth out, and narrowed his eyebrows. "Fear the Fang," he chanted, mispronouncing his own name. "Fear the Fang."

I was glad he was trying out.

Here's how I saw it. If he made the team, he wouldn't just be the geek Chinese kid who played the violin, designed eco-buildings, played chess, and got straight As. He'd be an athlete. Guys on the soccer team would walk down the hall with him, hang out with him before and after school. Hunter would back off. Athletes don't go after athletes.

When I reached the soccer field that afternoon, I

formed a circle with J. J. from weight training, Franklin Garcia from Algebra, both the McDermotts, and a bunch of other guys from Whitman. Richie came later, but he immediately joined us. Usually you can't tell much about a player from warm-ups, but with Richie I knew right away. Toe, heel, ankle, knee—it didn't matter. He had total control of the ball. When someone passed to him, he would do a couple of nifty moves and then pop the ball to someone else. He was a player.

After a few minutes, Coach Jacklin blew his whistle and called us all to him. I'd seen Jacklin around the campus. He had a round belly, his hair and clothes were always rumpled, and his eyes looked sleepy. But guys who played for him said that even though he looked like a beer-swilling slob, he knew soccer inside and out. They also said that he was fair—meaning freshmen could make the team if they were good enough.

Four of us were trying out for keeper. On that first day of tryouts, Coach Jacklin had told us that he was going to keep two goalies on varsity and send two to the JV team. "You're going to have to earn your spot. Nobody is given anything."

As we went through various drills, I sized up my competition at keeper. Reese Palmer, a freshman like me, had decent hands but was slow and short. He was JV material.

That left three of us fighting for two varsity spots.

Dustin Stoakes, a senior who had made the varsity team the year before, was a lock. If I was going to make varsity, I'd have to beat out Robby Cerac, a junior.

Cerac had the spiky hair and expensive clothes of the big soccer stars, and he had their cocky attitude, too. But he'd played JV, not varsity, the year before. Jacklin didn't know him much better than he knew me.

That first day, I dived for a ball and ended up flat on my belly in the mud. At the drinking fountain during a break, Cerac came over to me. "Skip the showboating. I paid my dues on the JV team last year, and that's where you're headed this year."

In the days before Richie, I'd have backed off, not wanting to make waves with a kid two years older than me. I'd have figured the JV team was good enough. But Richie had changed me.

He played soccer like he did everything else—all out. After one day, everyone knew he was going to make varsity. After day two, everyone knew he was going to start every game. After three days, we all knew he was our best player. If Richie was going to make the varsity team, then I wanted to make the varsity team. I wasn't going to hand anything to Cerac; he was going to have to beat me out.

CHAPTER 2

That week was windy, wet, and cold—what everybody thinks Seattle is like all the time. For five days, my hands were cold, my feet were cold, and my nose and ears were cold. The position guys could run to stay warm, but all the goalkeepers could do was hop up and down. Still, I fought to keep my focus, trying to play the way Richie played. Through every drill, I competed, diving for balls headed to the corner of the net, running out to cut down angles, making accurate passes and kicks.

Early on, Coach Jacklin had spent ten minutes with the four of us, explaining what he wanted in a keeper. "Be decisive. Don't freeze because you're worried about making a mistake." I paid attention to every word. So did Stoakes and Palmer, but Cerac spent the time kicking at the grass in front of him, looking bored.

On the last day of tryouts, we played a game. I shared time with Stoakes in the net for the white team, while

Cerac and Palmer traded off for the black. We rotated every ten minutes or so.

The game had barely begun—no more than ten seconds had gone by—when Cerac let a ball go right past him and into the net. He'd had his back turned and was pulling on his gloves. "That doesn't count," he shouted, grinning. "I didn't know we'd started." Guys laughed, but Coach Jacklin changed the score on his slate board from 0–0 to 1–0.

At halftime, Jacklin's slate still read 1–0. I'd made one good save and a half-dozen routine stops. Cerac, Stoakes, and Palmer had all done about the same.

I started the second half on the sidelines, but I was in goal with about ten minutes left in the game—and in the tryouts—when Richie, playing for the other team, took a ball at midfield, made a slick move to break free, and had twenty yards of green grass in front of him. He dribbled toward me, trying to make me commit. One of my guys was hustling back—I think it was Rory—taking the angle to cut him off. Richie saw Rory, stopped, and then ripped a shot on goal from about twenty-five yards.

The kick was chest high; I had a clear look at the ball. I moved to cut it off before it reached the goal, but it kept bending away. And it kept coming fast, too, not losing speed. At the last second, I laid out for the ball and felt it hit off my fingertips. I looked back and saw it cross over the end line just wide of the post.

"Great save!" Coach Jacklin shouted.

After the game, as Richie and I were about to head toward home, I heard Coach Jacklin call Cerac's name. We slowed and watched as the two talked. Cerac must have given Jacklin some lip, because Jacklin's face got red. Cerac said more, and then Jacklin said something that I couldn't hear. While he was still talking, Cerac turned his back on him and headed off the field, waving his hand above his head. "You can't put me on junior varsity," he yelled, turning back, "because I quit."

CHAPTER

A week before the soccer season started, the *Seattle Times* ran a preview of the league. When I came downstairs that morning, my father was at the table, finishing his coffee. "There's an article about your team," he said, sliding the newspaper toward me.

My eyes flew down the page. Coach Jacklin said we were his best team in years. *"We've got a great freshman class, kids that are used to winning,"* he'd told the reporter. *"We're going to surprise some teams this year."*

"That's you he's talking about," my dad said when I returned the newspaper to him. "You and the McDermotts and the other kids from Whitman. You guys are used to winning."

"It's Richie he's talking about."

My dad struggled to his feet, doing his best to hide

that he was struggling. "Richie Fang? Your do-everything friend?"

"Yeah. It turns out he plays soccer too. He can dribble, pass, shoot. And you wouldn't believe how far he can kick the ball. He's our best player."

As we rode over to our season-opening soccer game against the Roosevelt Roughriders, the defending city champions, Coach Jacklin still hadn't named his starting goalkeeper.

The bus pulled into the parking lot, and guys piled out. I was side by side with Richie, who was talking non-stop. Once I stepped off the bus, Jacklin motioned for me to wait. "You too, Dustin," he said.

Coach Jacklin waited for the other guys to move off before he spoke. "Boys, you have caused me some sleepless nights—you're that even. Here's what I've decided. Brock, you're going to start in goal." I tried to act calm, but my pulse went from eighty to one hundred eighty. I'd *done* it—I was the varsity goalkeeper.

And then I wasn't.

"But Dustin will take over in the second half. If one of you wins the job, then it's yours. But until then, you'll split the time. You two okay with that?" Dustin nodded his head and so did I. Jacklin smiled. "All right, then. Shut 'em out."

* * *

In a season opener, both teams usually start out tentative, but there was nothing tentative about Richie's play. He spent most of his time on the offensive side, pushing the ball hard and then looking to make a touch pass into the scoring zone. Most soccer plays fail—that's just the way it is. After a good run that crashes, lots of guys drop their head and mope, at least for a few seconds, but Richie always hustled back, immediately looking to stop any counterattack.

In the twentieth minute, Peter Lee, one of our wingers, raced upfield on the right side as Richie came up the middle. Richie had twice made spot-on passes to Lee, but this time he faked the pass and then blasted a shot from twenty yards. The goalie was slow to react, so all he could do was watch as the ball slammed into the upper-left-hand corner of the net. While the other guys on our team chased after him, Richie raced around in a semicircle, a huge grin on his face, screaming, "Fear the Fang!" and shooting imaginary six-guns. He made the whole thing into wild fun, though I don't think the Roosevelt players saw it that way.

After our goal, Roosevelt pressed the attack. For the next ten minutes, the ball lived on our side, but Richie and the McDermott twins slowed the breakaways, made steals, and boomed the ball downfield out of the scoring zone. Still, their pressure stayed on.

Finally we made a mistake—Peter mishandled what should have been a pass across the middle. A Roosevelt forward took control of the ball and made a clever move past Tim. Suddenly two Roughriders were coming at me. Pass—pass—shoot! I had a clear view, so I saw the ball all the way. At the right moment, I leaped, just as I'd leaped for a pass from Hunter. The ball slammed hard into my hands, but I hung on. On the sidelines, Coach Jacklin jumped up and down, and Dustin stuck two fingers in his mouth and whistled. I booted the ball to the right side and returned to the net. Then I thought of my dad.

I wished he had seen that play.

My save took the fire out of Roosevelt for the rest of the half. Right before halftime, Richie stole a sloppy pass and was off. A few yards outside the box, he fired a ball toward Peter, leaving him with a point-blank shot that no one could miss. Peter didn't, pushing our lead to 2–0.

During the break, Jacklin's jaw was tight. "I've lost to these guys eight straight times. I'm so sick of their coach saying 'Nice game' in that smug way of his that if I hear it again today, I swear to God I'll smack him in the face. So you'd better finish these guys or your coach will end up in jail."

Dustin took my spot in goal for the second half. I

didn't like it—no one wants to come out of a game—but I'd done my part.

Down by two goals, Roosevelt had to keep taking chances. You take risks, you risk getting burned. Rory scored on a breakaway, pushing our lead to 3–0, and that's how the game ended.

CHAPTER 4

Anya had stopped her campaign against the coal train and had switched to a Yes Means Yes campaign. It was anti-rape stuff, so she didn't ask any guys to sit at the table with her. That was okay by me. Rape is not something I wanted to talk about.

The day after the Roosevelt game, she told me about the party. "For Pie Day," she said. "You know. Friday is Pie Day."

I looked at her blankly.

"Three point one four. Pi. If you write it as a calendar day, it comes out as March fourteenth. I know it's kind of nerdy, but Friday night we're going to bake some pies and then eat them. You want to come?"

"Yeah, sure," I said, trying to hide my eagerness. "What time?"

"Eight or so."

When I knocked on her door, Anya answered and led

me into the kitchen, where two other kids were standing around a table. There were three pie shells on the table, and bowls of cut-up apples, frozen strawberries, and canned cherries. "I have to pat the shells down," Anya said, "and then we can spoon the good stuff in."

I didn't know the other kids, so Anya introduced me. The girl, a tall blonde, who was on the basketball team, was Leslie. The guy's name was Elon. They were both older, at least sophomores, maybe juniors. I figured they were in Symonds's class, too.

Elon was standing right next to Leslie, shoulder to shoulder, hip to hip. They were a pair. I went over to Anya's side of the table and helped spoon the fruit into the shells. Next, Anya rolled out more pastry dough and explained how to make a latticed top.

Once the pies were in the oven, we went downstairs into a basement rec room. Mainly the conversation was about Symonds's class. That was okay, though. I could just nod my head and not have to worry that I'd say something stupid.

Two of the pies were great, but we forgot to put sugar in the one with cherries, so it tasted terrible. Anya had a can of whipped cream, and we took turns making mounds on top of our pieces of pie. "It looks like a perfectly shaped female breast," Elon said when he finished his, and Leslie whacked him in the arm.

We each ate two pieces of pie and then went back

downstairs. After a few minutes, Anya's younger brother, Sam, joined us. Anya tried to chase him away, but he ignored her and set up a golf game on a Wii. "Who wants to play?" he asked once the screen came to life.

Elon shook his head. "Not me."

My dad had taught me a little about how to swing a golf club, which made me an expert in that room. "I'll play," I said.

Sam knew less about golf than I did. We played three holes, and I thrashed him. When we finished, Anya jumped up. "Show me how to swing," she said.

Her brother handed her the controls. I stood behind her and reached my arms around her. My hands were on her arms, close to her breasts. My face was close to her face.

Just then the door flew open, her father stepped into the room, and we both froze. He stared at us. "You stop that," he ordered.

Anya and I jumped apart. Her face turned bright red. "He was just showing me how to play golf on the Wii."

Her father glared at me. "He can show somebody else."

When her father went back upstairs, we stayed motionless for a long moment, and then we all burst out laughing, including Anya, though her face stayed bright red. Mine was burning too.

CHAPTER

For a while, everything was good. My father was doing better, or at least not getting worse. Richie's mother was getting stronger, and Hunter and Colton had stopped hassling Richie. I'd been right: Athletes don't hassle other athletes.

And Richie was an athlete. Against Franklin, he made a great pass with a back header. In the Garfield game, he bent a corner kick like Beckham, just like he said he could, and Peter headed it in. Richie was nearly as fast with the ball as without it and—even though he was small—he never let guys out-muscle him on contested balls.

It's weird: not many kids play football, but lots of kids go to football games. With soccer, it's just the opposite. Everybody plays; nobody goes, except parents and girlfriends. Still, news of our victories spread through the school. Crown Hill hadn't had a first-place team in any sport for years, so a top-notch soccer team was a big deal, which meant that Richie was a big deal.

Richie never bragged about how good he was in music or chess or math, but he bragged like crazy about his soccer feats. His voice was loud as he described his wondrous plays to anyone who was listening and to lots of kids who weren't. As he talked, he spread his arms wide and his cheeks went rosy. "Fear the Fang!" he'd say when his story came to an end. "Fear the Fang!"

We didn't win every game. That just doesn't happen in soccer. We hit a spell where no breaks went our way, but even then our team won three games, tied two, and lost only one. I gave up a couple of goals, but none of them were cheap. All season long, we were either in first or second place.

The cheer team stuck posters celebrating our victories in the main entranceway to the school. And Mr. Spady, in the morning announcements, gave the final score and the names of anybody who'd had a goal or an assist. Kids in the hallway or at lunch would see Richie and chant "Fear the Fang." Whenever that happened, Richie would raise his hands above his head, boxer style, and try to look fierce, which just made kids laugh more.

It was all good.

Then the Suzanne Friend stuff happened.

I'd known Suzanne since kindergarten. She lived with her mother in a small brown house halfway between my home and Gilman Park. Nobody ever used the word *retard* in front of teachers, but that's the word that got used when teachers weren't around.

Beginning in second grade, Suzanne spent the mornings in the special ed room for reading, writing, and math. In the afternoons, she was in regular classes like art and social studies. Nobody thought much about her. She was just a slightly strange girl who spent most of the day in special ed.

Then, in middle school, she got breasts. She got them before any of the other girls. Beautiful breasts. Movie star breasts.

In middle school, girls with no breasts at all wore bras, but Suzanne didn't. You could see her breasts moving as she walked, her nipples poking against her too-small T-shirts.

Eventually Suzanne figured out that boys were staring at her body. Other girls didn't like being stared at, but Suzanne did. Probably it was the first time anyone paid attention to her, the first time she had anything on the other girls.

In high school, it was more of the same, only now the guys staring at her were bolder, and she was bolder too. Once, she caught me eyeing her. She smiled. "You like them, don't you?" And then she shook her breasts, a big smile on her face. I watched them move under her shirt, and she laughed.

She shook them for lots of guys. Every time she did it for me, I felt guilty. I never once asked her to do it, and she seemed to like it, but watching her didn't feel right.

A couple of times I saw Ms. Kater, the school nurse, pull Suzanne aside to talk to her. After that, she'd wear a bra for a while and she wouldn't shake for guys, but eventually it would start again.

At first, Hunter didn't pay much attention to her. Then, one day, he pretended to be her boyfriend. I wasn't there, but I heard how he wrapped his arm around her and told her that she was his girl. After that, whenever he saw her he'd say, "You know what I like, Suzanne." She'd smile and shake. He'd tell her she was his girl and kiss her while all his buddies smirked.

Richie was with me once when Hunter pulled this. It was right after lunch and I just wanted to get away to my next class, but Richie stayed rooted.

Suzanne was moving this way and that, belly-dancing in a way, but she was so uncoordinated that it really wasn't a dance. Some kids were snickering, but most kids were pushing by, trying to get away. "This is not right," Richie said. "Somebody should stop him."

The warning bell rang. "You're my sweetheart forever," Hunter said, and then kissed her dramatically on the lips like you see in old-time movies—Suzanne folded back into a reverse C and Hunter pressed against her while his friends punched each other and swallowed their laughter. I pulled a third time on Richie's arm, and he finally followed me away.

A few days later, a rumor started going around that Hunter was taking Suzanne behind the gym at lunch and having her lift up her shirt so he could see and feel her breasts. Some kids said he did way more.

I didn't know how much was true, but the thought of it made me sick. I'm not saying I didn't want to feel a girl's breasts, but not a girl like Suzanne Friend. Not a girl who didn't know what was going on.

One day—it was the day after we'd played to a tie with Cleveland that left us in second place—the school was in an uproar. I saw Tim McDermott in the hallway, and he told me that someone had reported Hunter Gates to Mr. Spady. "They know about him and Suzanne Friend."

"Who told?" I asked.

"Nobody knows."

I pulled Richie aside at soccer practice. "Did you do it?" I whispered.

"Do what?"

"Turn in Hunter Gates?"

His face screwed up in confusion. "What are you talking about?"

I explained. "It wasn't me," he said when I finished. "I'm glad somebody did, but it wasn't me."

Both Hunter and Suzanne were absent from school the next day. Word was that the special ed teacher, Ms. Levine, had them in Mr. Spady's office all morning. In the afternoon, Ms. Levine came around to classrooms. "If you see something that's wrong, have the courage to speak up," she said, her eyes on fire.

She never used Suzanne's name or Hunter's name. Some kids were clueless, but most kids knew what she was talking about. As Ms. Levine spoke, I thought about the times I'd watched Suzanne shake, and I stared at my desktop.

The next morning, Suzanne was back at school. She was wearing a bra, had on a loose-fitting shirt, and kept her head down as she moved through the hall. I thought Hunter might have gotten suspended, but around lunchtime I saw him. He was walking the way he normally walked, a little smile on his face.

"He didn't force her to do anything," I heard J.J. say. "She wanted to do it. Ms. Levine can get all bent out of shape, but she can't do anything to Hunter. He didn't break any laws."

CHAPTER 6

The Puget Sound Chess Association held a tournament just before spring break. Anya was the second-to-last person chosen, and I was the last, so for all the games I was sitting next to her. I did okay, winning two and losing two.

The individual championship was the final match of the day. Richie and some guy from the Lakeside School sat on stage, and their game was projected onto a huge screen so everyone could watch. I was certain Richie would win—who could ever beat him at anything?—so I was blown away when the Lakeside kid demolished him in ten minutes. As far as I knew, Richie had never lost at anything.

Mr. Gupta had driven the six of us to the tournament in a school district van. On the ride back, Richie was quiet for the first few minutes. I could tell he was replaying the championship game in his mind. Then Richie nodded his head up and down a few times. "He was really, really good."

On Monday, Richie was announced as the second-place finisher in the chess contest, and his trophy was displayed in the trophy case outside the gym. At lunch, the photographer for the school newspaper took his picture. Richie, grinning broadly, held the trophy with his right hand and flashed the victory sign with his left. "I'm number two!" he shouted.

A couple of nights later, I got a phone call from Rory. "Hey, Brock, I thought you should know," he said. "It was your new friend, that Fang kid, who told Spady about Suzanne Friend and Hunter."

"Who says that?"

"Fang says it. Hunter was nosing around, trying to find out who'd ratted him out, and Fang just went up to him and said that he'd done it, and that he was glad he had. The guy's got balls. He's stupid, but he's got balls."

"But he didn't do it. I'm sure he didn't."

Rory snorted. "Well, if he didn't, why would he say he did?"

Before school the next morning I found Richie in a corner of the cafeteria reading a book on math puzzles. I pulled my chair up next to him. "I heard what you did, but you don't have to be a hero. Let the person who turned Hunter in take the flak. It's their problem, not yours."

"It's not that simple."

"It is that simple."

"What if I told you it was Anya?"

As soon as he said her name, I knew it was true. Anya had no fear of anyone, and she'd stand up for Suzanne.

The clock ticked off ten seconds, then ten seconds more. Something was wrong, but what? Then another thought came to me. "It won't work, Richie. Anya won't go along. She'll say she did it."

He shrugged. "And I'll say she's lying to protect me. Hunter will believe it was me. Everyone will believe it."

I knew immediately he was right.

The bell rang. I stood, my head pounding. "You're going to have to be really careful."

He smiled a totally fake smile. "Don't worry about me, Brock. I possess the strength of five Bruce Lees. *Fear the Fang!*"

CHAPTER 7

I don't know all that went down after that. Nobody but Richie knows. I do know that most of what happened was small stuff, that it was sometimes done by Hunter, sometimes by his friends.

First somebody stole Richie's shoes during gym class and threw them onto the roof of the greenhouse. Then dog crap was smeared on the outside of his locker. Guys knocked into him in the hallways, especially in Suicide Alley, or slapped books and papers out of his hands as they walked by. Richie would go to sit down in class or in the commons, and somebody would pull his chair out from under him.

Stupid junk like that, but over and over.

Richie ignored Hunter, ignored all guys who were harassing him. He was still smiling at practice, still saying crazy things. "Once there was a guy on my team who had an extra finger on each hand. After he scored a goal, we all shouted, 'Gimme six!'" But if you knew him—and I did—you could see in his eyes that the jokes were covers.

Somehow, he kept playing great. No Crown Hill soccer team had made it to the state tournament in decades, but as the victories mounted we started thinking that—if Richie kept being Richie—we could break through. The cheer team took down the old posters about the soccer team and replaced them with a bunch of newly painted ones that read FEAR THE FANG! in red letters. They hung posters above the doors of the school. They put more in the library windows, and a couple outside the gym. Everywhere you went, you saw FEAR THE FANG!

When Richie first saw one of the posters, he stared at it for a while and then nudged me and pointed. "I wish they'd drawn fangs growing out of the *G*. That would have been cool."

"Tell them. Maybe they'll do it."

He waved me off. "No. If they take them down, they might not get them up again."

I was afraid that Richie would carry some of the garbage going on at school onto the soccer field, but his game stayed strong. After we beat Franklin 2–0 on a cold, windy Friday night, we needed just one more victory—over Lakeside, on their field—to make it into the state tournament. It would be our toughest game of the year, but we had magic going. Everything seemed possible.

CHAPTER 0

I heard about it before I saw it. A guy from my history class, Nick Spadoni, called out to me as I was walking up the steps to school on Monday morning. "Did you see what they did?"

I felt my pulse slow and the blood drain from my head, making me weak and dizzy. I didn't know what he was talking about, but I knew who "they" were.

"You won't like it," Spadoni went on, an odd expression on his face, as if he knew he shouldn't smile but was struggling to keep from smiling. "Follow me. I'll show you."

He led me inside the main entrance of the school and told me to look back at it. All I saw were the main doors with kids coming through them. "What?" I said, turning back to him.

He pointed. "Up there."

I followed his finger until my eyes rested on the big FEAR THE FANG poster. Only now it didn't read FEAR THE FANG! A big X had been drawn over the *N*. To the right was a poster-size Photoshopped picture of Richie. Whoever did it gave him chipmunk cheeks, superslanty eyes, a Chinese afro, and an idiotic toothy grin.

I turned on Spadoni. The blood that had drained from my head was surging back, and now it was boiling. "Don't get mad at me, Brock," he said, holding up his hands in a sign of surrender. "I didn't do it."

Kids around me were looking up. "That's mean," somebody said, but other kids were laughing.

My eyes returned to Spadoni. "Has anybody reported this?"

He shrugged. "How should I know?"

I pushed past him and hurried to the main office. Ms. O'Neill was behind her desk, typing. "Do you know about—"

"Yes," she said, not looking up. "We've got a call in to get them taken down."

"Them? Did they do it to all of them?"

"I don't know about all of them, but most of them."

"How come they're not down already?"

Now she did look up. "There's a substitute custodian today, and he can't find a ladder."

"They've got to come down right now. You can't let them stay up."

She tilted her head and glared. "Do you know where the ladder is?"

"No." I shot back.

"We're moving as fast as we can. But nothing can happen until we find the ladder."

Richie wasn't at English class. During chess club, Anya told me that when he'd come in the main entryway that morning, everyone there had gone completely quiet. When he looked up, he stared at the sign for a while and then walked out the door, down the steps, and off campus. "I've texted him a couple of times, but he hasn't answered," Anya said. "I hope he's okay."

"He's tough," I told her. "Tougher than anyone I've ever met. These guys can't break him."

"It's racist, you know," she said, after a long moment. "All of it. If he were black, or Hispanic, or white like you, they wouldn't do it. But Asians? Anybody can make fun of Asians. So they make that poster and stick it up all over the school. They call him a fag and that's funny too. You think we're machines, robots, that we study too hard and get too many As. You think we'll take it because we're too polite to fight back, because Asians don't make trouble."

"*I* don't think that way!" I said.

"Don't you?" she snapped. She glared at me for a moment and then abruptly stood. "I don't feel like playing chess today," she said, and then she walked out, leaving me staring at sixty-four black and white squares.

CHAPTER 9

Richie wasn't at practice that day. Coach Jacklin had warned us that anyone with an unexcused absence from school or practice would be suspended for a game.

Without Richie on the field, practice was lifeless. It was as if we were responsible for what had happened. We were so bad that Coach Jacklin cut practice short. I went home, ate dinner, and then called Richie. He didn't answer, so I sent him a text message. He didn't reply.

Mr. Spady had to know Hunter was behind the posters. Would he have the guts to do anything about it?

Before school the next day, I looked for Richie, but I couldn't find him. All through first period, crazy thoughts swirled in my head, like that he'd transfer to a different school and I'd never see him again. But when I stepped into Ms. Ringleman's room, Richie was in his usual spot.

He acted as if everything was normal, so I pretended

nothing had happened too. I slumped into the empty desk next to him and asked if some strippers had tried to take my spot. He shook his head. "No strippers."

Class started. We'd been reading a short story about a kid in Palestine who started out one morning with a new bicycle and made a series of idiotic trades and came home at the end of the day with a pencil sharpener. The kid in the story was crazy/funny in a way that reminded me of Richie. The normal Richie would have had a lot to say about the story, but he didn't raise his hand once.

When class ended, he was out the door before I even had my backpack zipped. I didn't see him at lunch or at chess club. I worried that he'd quit the soccer team, but when I stepped on the field I saw him huddled with Coach Jacklin. Jacklin had both hands on Richie's shoulders, which is what my dad used to do when he really wanted my attention. I always looked right in my dad's eyes when he did that—I just had to—but Richie's head was turning this way and that, his eyes looking everywhere but at Coach Jacklin. When their talk ended, Richie wandered over to where the rest of us were warming up.

"What was that about?" I asked.

"I can play."

"That's great."

"Yeah," he said, his voice cold. "Great." Then he moved off to warm up with other guys.

All through practice, he was like a downed electric wire—alive and dangerous. His intensity kept everybody on the team focused. Ball movement, dribbling, and defense—it was all top-notch, but nobody took any joy in it. Our practices had been fun because Richie had always been shouting out some crazy joke or making some off-the-wall comment. Now he was stone-faced, so the rest of us were stone-faced too.

There was a difference in how he played, too. He'd always been physical, but now he crossed the line. Forearms to the back, slide tackles that were borderline trips, elbows to the ribs on long runs. "Watch it, Richie," Jasper Hastings, a senior fullback, said after one rough play that Coach Jacklin hadn't seen.

"Watch it yourself," Richie snapped back.

Hastings took a step toward Richie, and Richie stepped right up in his face. Jacklin spotted the two of them and started blowing his whistle like a crazy man. "Save it for Lakeside," Jacklin shouted, rushing over.

The next day, during sixth period, Mr. Spady called me to his office and had me sit in a plastic chair across from his huge desk. He folded his hands in front of him. "You're good friends with Richie Fang, right?"

I nodded.

"How's he doing?"

I shrugged. "He's not saying much, but he's got to be boiling inside."

Mr. Spady sighed. "I don't blame him. Big joke. Ha ha."

The room fell quiet. "Hunter Gates did it," I said, breaking the silence. "You know that, don't you?"

Mr. Spady shook his head. "Hunter was skiing at Steven's Pass all weekend. Colton was with him. They didn't get back until Sunday night."

"Who says?" I asked, not hiding my disbelief.

Spady's voice sharpened. "Hunter's father. He was with them the whole time."

I thought for a moment. "Then Hunter did it Sunday night after he came back. It wouldn't take long."

Spady shook his head. "Impossible. The custodians locked the school at eight Saturday night, and it stayed locked until Monday morning. There's an alarm system. Nobody got in this building on Sunday."

Again the room fell silent. Finally, Mr. Spady leaned toward me, his voice kinder. "Look, Brock, I know you want whoever did this punished. So do I. But right now, Richie's mental state is the most important thing. The school district has a professional counselor available for situations like this. She could help Richie."

I shook my head. "He won't see a counselor. No way."

"That's what he told me when I had him in here. But I still think it would be good for him, and I think that if you backed me up, he might change his mind."

"So that's why I'm here. You want me to talk to Richie about seeing a counselor."

"Yes, I do."

I shook my head. "Hunter Gates did this. Suspend him or expel him. Just do something. That would help Richie."

Spady sat up straight. His voice was all business. "Brock, I told you. Hunter wasn't involved. So get rid of that idea. It's a dead end."

We had no practice that day. Coach Jacklin wanted us to rest so we'd have fresh legs for the game. After school, I stopped by Richie's house. He was in the shed working on his model. We talked about the upcoming soccer game, acting as if everything were normal. Finally, I told him about Spady calling me in.

"And Spady believes the ski story?" he asked.

"What can he do? He's not going to call Mr. Gates a liar, and he's not going to hire some private eye to investigate."

"How about you?" Richie said. "Do you believe it?"

"No," I said, then paused. "But I suppose there's a chance it wasn't Hunter."

Richie shrugged. "Yeah, I guess."

He turned his attention back to his model, putting up lampposts and straightening trees. We worked together in silence for about ten minutes. Then, completely out of nowhere, he asked me if I had a gun. "I don't mean you. I mean your dad. Does he have one?"

"Are you kidding? He'd never have a gun in the house."

"My father has one. It's right there." He pointed to a mahogany box on a shelf next to some pruners. "When we first came here from Nanjing, my dad believed that every American was a millionaire and that every American kept a gun in his house. So he bought a Browning Hi Power pistol, the best pistol ever made. That's how he is. If you're going to get something, get the best." He took a step toward the shelf. "Do you want to hold it? It's a work of art. It feels perfect in your hand. The design is incredible."

I put my hands up. "I don't want to touch it. Guns freak me out."

"At least look at it." He reached up, took down the box, and opened it. "Isn't it beautiful? The muzzle, the handle, the trigger, the way the magazine fits in—everything about it is perfect."

"Except for what it does. That's not so perfect."

He took it out of the box.

"Put it back, Richie. I don't like it."

He looked at me, shrugged, and then put it back in the box. "It's not loaded. The magazine clip is in the house.

My dad hides it in a bottom drawer in the bathroom." He grinned. "It's in a box with a label that reads POISON, DO NOT OPEN. If he hadn't put that sign on the box, I'd never have looked inside."

CHAPTER 10

My father hadn't gone to my soccer games. After each match, I'd play radio announcer, telling him everything. That's what I figured I'd do for the final game, but he insisted on attending in person. "I'm not missing the game that could send you to the state championship," he said, his voice firm.

I felt sick. I knew nothing about the layout of Lakeside High. If it was a long walk from the parking lot to the bleachers, it would take him forever, with everybody watching. He'd hate that, and I hated the idea of my teammates seeing him struggle.

His voice dropped. "Don't worry, Brock. The field is down in a hollow; First Avenue runs right above it. I can park by the fence and see the game better than if I were sitting in the bleachers."

The team took a school bus to Lakeside. Every other bus ride had been loosey-goosey, because Richie had set the tone. Before the bus had even pulled out of the parking lot, he'd be telling some crazy story. Guys would laugh and then tell their own stories. This time, Richie sat by himself in the back of the bus and stared out the window.

Pulling onto the Lakeside campus was like entering a different world. Bill Gates—the billionaire Bill Gates, not Hunter's father—had gone there. I've never seen Harvard or Yale, but Lakeside looked the way I imagine them to look. Brick buildings with ivy crawling up the sides, a big quad bordered with flower beds and crisscrossed with cobblestone paths, wrought-iron benches underneath shade trees. I half expected a security guard to stop our bus, ask us what we were doing there, and then tell us to go away.

Rich kids have a huge advantage in sports like soccer. In the off-season, guys on my team played in rec leagues or maybe on select teams. Lakeside kids play year-round in premier leagues, getting the best coaching while traveling the world to take on the best competition.

At game time, we had a couple dozen parents in the bleachers on our side. I looked to the street above the field to see if I could find my dad's van. I spotted it, and him, and gave a wave.

From the start, Richie was a ticking bomb. I saw it, and so did Coach Jacklin. Twice I heard him holler, "Easy, easy" to Richie, urging him to get the play under control. If it had been anybody else, Jacklin would have yanked him, but we had no chance to win with Richie on the bench.

For a while, Richie's over-the-top intensity worked in our favor. The Lakeside guys backed off when they saw him rushing upfield. It was as if they were jumping out of the path of a speeding car. We were the aggressive team, moving the ball from side to side, looking for chances.

Their goalie made a good save on a shot from the left side, and a couple of minutes later Richie made a corner kick that almost found the net. A minute after that, Rickie boomed a shot, but it flew just wide.

But another chance came right away. Rory stole the ball and led Richie with a perfect pass. Richie took it and dribbled upfield. He had Peter open on the side and could have passed it to him. Instead, he tried to deke a Lakeside fullback. It was a smart play; if he got past him, it would be clear sailing to the goal.

But the Lakeside guys were players. The fullback ran shoulder to shoulder with Richie before making a beautiful steal, poking the ball away without touching Richie. It was an amazing play, and the Lakeside fans roared their approval.

A Lakeside kid chased down the ball, turned it, and was moving upfield. The kid was running easy, surveying the field, looking for someone to pass to. There wasn't a play set up. Nothing.

Suddenly, Richie raced at the kid from behind. I don't know what he was thinking, but he had no angle. That was bad. Worse, Richie had his cleats up when he tried his slide tackle, or whatever it was. He never touched the ball, but he did hit the back of the Lakeside guy's leg. The kid's knee buckled and he went down hard. You could hear everybody in the stands—on both sides—gasp. A second later, the Lakeside player started rolling over and over, howling in pain as he clutched his knee.

The ref blew long and hard on his whistle, and a trainer or doctor rushed onto the field. Players for both teams kneeled as the doctor guy bent over the Lakeside kid. He moved his leg a little, then a little more, and then he was up, grimacing as he hobbled to the sidelines, blood dripping down his leg and onto his shoe and sock. The parents and kids in the stands clapped for him.

After that, a bunch of things happened, one after the other like a string of firecrackers exploding. Lakeside dads started pointing their fingers and screaming at Richie. "Get that kid off the field," one of them shouted in a booming voice.

The ref motioned Richie to him. He talked to Richie for about thirty seconds, and then the red card came out and he pointed to the sidelines. The Lakeside parents cheered.

Coach Jacklin came out and walked Richie off the

field. Angry shouts from the Lakeside section followed him every step.

There was an old gray blanket on the bench. When Richie sat down, Jacklin grabbed that blanket and placed it over Richie's shoulders. Richie immediately pulled it over his head, put his knees on his elbows, and fixed his eyes on the grass by his feet.

There's not much to say about the rest of the game. Our best player had been ejected; we were short-handed; we were playing on Lakeside's field; we were completely off our game. Because of Richie's foul, we wanted to prove we were good sports, so we played politely, which is another way of saying we played soft. On top of that, they were the better team, even when we'd had Richie. The final score was 6–0.

Season over.

Riding back to school on the bus, Richie sat by himself in the first row. Behind him on both sides for two rows were empty seats. I could have sat next to him, stuck by him and all that, but what could I have said that would have been of any use?

When the bus doors hissed open in the school parking lot, Richie was off the bus first. By the time I made my way to the front, he was half a block away. That was okay. I didn't want to walk home with him. Not that day.

My dad was waiting for me when I opened the front door. "Some things just aren't meant to be," he said, giving me a shake of the head and a half smile. "Still, you had a great year." There was a long pause. "What's going on with your friend Richie? That was a terrible foul. Where'd that come from?"

I still think about that moment. My dad was right in front of me, asking. I could have told him everything—about Richie's mom being sick, about Suzanne Friend, about Fear the Fag, about Hunter and all the crap he and his friends had pulled.

"He just made a stupid play," I said. "That's all."

CHAPTER 11

Richie wasn't at school Monday or Tuesday. I thought about stopping by his house to see how he was doing, but I figured he wanted time to himself.

Coach Jacklin called a team meeting Tuesday at lunch. As we were waiting, guys around me talked about Richie, how he'd cost us a chance at the playoffs, how dirty his play had been, how they weren't surprised he wasn't at school. "I'd stay home too, if I'd pissed away our chances," one guy said.

"He should be here," somebody else put in. "He screwed up bigtime, and he should man up."

When other guys nodded in agreement, I'd had enough. "Give the guy a break, will you?" I said to no one and to everyone. "Without Richie, we'd have done nothing. And what would you have done if those posters had been about you?"

After my outburst, guys looked at the ground or out

the window. Everybody was glad when Jacklin arrived so we could listen to his "It was a great year" speech and be done with the soccer season.

When I stepped inside Ms. Ringleman's room on Wednesday, I spotted Richie in the last row between two kids who always slept through class. There were no empty desks near him. Our eyes met, and I motioned to some vacant seats up front, hoping he'd move, but he shook his head. At lunch I looked around for him, but he'd found a table way in the back that was full of Asian kids, and he ignored me when I pointed to where we normally ate. I don't know where he went after lunch, but it wasn't to chess club.

Over the next weeks, I tried to break through, and sometimes I thought I had. There'd be an open seat next to him in Ms. Ringleman's class, and I'd take it. We'd talk a little before class, and sometimes even eat lunch together. But he was shut up tight. He didn't want me, or anyone, around.

As a kid, I'd owned some of those transformer toys where you had a tank and then you flipped a few arms and it turned into a fighter jet. He was like that. The joking, outgoing Richie had morphed into a head-down, never-smile kid.

Maybe that's why Hunter and his friends started getting on him again. Colton started calling Richie "Red"—short for Red Card—and lots of kids thought tagging a black-haired Asian kid with the nickname Red was funny. "Hey, there's Red," guys would say as he walked down the hallway, and they could use that name even if teachers were around. Same thing with MVP. At least twice, at the end of the day a group of guys followed him off campus, chanting, *"MVP! MVP! MVP!"*—mocking him for getting himself kicked out of the Lakeside game.

Whenever anybody I knew ridiculed Richie, I told them to knock it off, and most of the time they did. But not always.

"I don't know why you keep defending him," Rory shot back me at one day in the lunchroom. "He screwed up. And he was always bragging about how great he was. You puff yourself up like that and you're asking for somebody to smack you down."

I picked up my tray and moved to another table. "The truth hurts," Rory called after me, but I didn't look back.

CHAPTER 12

On the last Friday in May, school let out early so that teachers could get training on new tests we'd have to take next year. At eleven, I started for home, not sure what I'd do to kill the afternoon. About ten blocks from my house, I decided to stop by Richie's. If he didn't want me around, he'd let me know.

When I neared his house, I could tell things had gone bad. The grass hadn't been mowed; the flower beds were full of weeds. As I came closer, things looked even worse. The hanging plants on the porch were dead; cobwebs traced paths from the porch light; bits of trash had blown up against the fence.

From the sidewalk, I could see a light on in the kitchen, and I thought I heard music. I climbed the porch stairs and knocked on the front door. I waited. Nothing. I was about to knock again when Richie's mother opened the door.

She looked older and weaker. She smiled when she saw me, but even smiling seemed like it was work for her. "Oh, it's you, Richie's friend. I'm so glad you come. Richie is around back, working on ecology school. You go there; you find him."

I thanked her and then walked through the gate to the shed. It still seemed deserted—was his mother wrong? "Richie, are you in there?"

The door opened. Richie was holding a tube of Super Glue in one hand, a tiny park bench in the other, and he had earphones around his neck. For a minute, he just stared at me, not even saying hello. Then he stepped aside. "Come in."

My eyes immediately went to the model of the school. I couldn't believe what I was looking at. All the sports fields were finished, and they were perfect. The football field had yardage lines every five yards. The baseball and softball diamonds had tiny bases in perfect position around the tiny infield. The creek running through the school was lined with miniature benches and picnic tables. Thumb-size people ate pea-size meals under a line of shade trees.

"It's *awesome*," I said.

"Yeah, well, this is all I've been working on for a while, so it should be good." He pointed to a bare spot. "That'll be a new wing for the school heated entirely by solar panels. I worked out the economics of it. Even in

Seattle there's enough sunlight to heat a building that size if you have enough glass and you position the building just right. For the contest, you have to prove that your concept works; you can't just make up stuff."

"You're going to win," I said. "Not just in Portland, but for the whole country. Nothing else could be this good."

He screwed up his face and sort of smiled. "Maybe. But some kid in Eugene might have done twice as much. You never know."

We stared silently at the model for a long moment.

"Did you go to the front door? Did see my mother?" he asked.

"Yeah, I saw her."

"Her cancer is back. She cries all the time. My father yells at her not to give up, but that makes her cry more, and that makes him yell more. That's why I come out here and lock the door."

My mouth went dry. "But the doctors are still treating her, right?"

"Yeah, they're treating her, but it won't work."

"Don't say that, Richie. You don't know that."

"It's true. I looked it up online. Chemo never works the second time. Or almost never. And I heard my father on the phone. He's already arranging our move back to Nanjing so my aunts can raise me. I told him I want to stay here, but he won't listen."

"Something could still happen, Richie. You just don't know."

He laughed. "Yeah, sure. Something could happen. Twenty-three cockatiels could fly around my room and poop on my head. Big-breasted girls could beg to sit next to me."

A few seconds ticked by. Then I smiled. "Hey, those big-breasted girls have got to sit next to somebody. Why not you?"

His face stayed stony. "This isn't a joke, Brock."

"Come on, Richie. I was just trying to— " I stopped. The words wouldn't come.

"Trying to what?"

"I don't know. Forget it." I paused. "Do you want me to go?"

He sighed, and his face relaxed. "No. I'm sick of working on this alone. If you want to stick around and help, that'd be great."

CHAPTER 13

Spring football started June 1. Not that many guys turned out. All the seniors—including J'Varre—were done with high school football. The incoming freshmen were still back in middle school, and some guys had quit. That left about fifty players on the field.

Coach Payne called us together. The assistant coaches were standing on one side, the parent volunteers on the other. He talked for a while, and then turned toward his assistants.

"I want you men to meet Coach Lever. You may have seen him around school; he teaches P.E. and biology. I'll be here to help with the transition this week, but in the fall Coach Lever will be your head coach. I've had a good long run, but this is it for me. Any questions?"

We all stood silent, too stunned to speak. There couldn't have been a more different coach. Coach Payne was an old white guy with bags under his eyes. He had as much hair growing out of his ears as he had on his head. I'd seen him smile a couple of times but never laugh. Coach Lever was a young black guy, built like an NBA player and tatted up like one too. He wore tiny diamond earrings, and in the hallways he was always smiling, always upbeat. He'd come to Crown Hill in January when one of the lady P.E. teachers had had a baby.

Somebody shouted out, "We'll miss you, Coach!" Coach Payne smiled and nodded his head and said he'd miss us, too. Then we all clapped for him, and the guys who knew how to whistle did, and the changeover started.

Coach Lever brought a new style to the team. As we warmed up, rap music blared from speakers placed all around the field. 2Pac and Eminem and the Beastie Boys. When we switched to hitting the sleds, he played old heavy metal: Led Zeppelin and Guns N' Roses and AC/DC.

Coach Payne looked disgusted as the music blared. Some of the other coaches and the parent volunteers were rolling with it; some of them looked like they might walk off.

But for us, the players? It was great. The music got the blood going, and we needed that, because Coach Lever worked us really hard. We ran more, hit the sleds more, and did more drills than at Coach Payne's practices. The music somehow made you want to run. That and Coach Lever's nonstop cheerleading. "Gimme more, white boy," he screamed at me once, a smile on his face. And I gave him more. We all did.

When we broke into small groups, I was with the other receivers and the quarterbacks. Kaiden had quit, but Aiden was there with Hunter. As he threw easy passes to us—it was the first day—I saw something different in Hunter. He was never a screw-off on the football field, but that day he was even more intense. The upcoming season was his last chance. More mediocre play and he'd be lucky to get a scholarship offer from a Division III school like Pacific Lutheran.

For two hours, we worked hard. Coach Payne had directed practice from his high platform; Coach Lever ran from offensive group to defensive group, clapping his hands and asking for more effort.

At the end of practice, he had us form a circle. "You guys got to get your own rap," he said. "Every good team has one. So come on, loosen up, find your voice."

I'd seen teams do that. They'd get in a circle and somebody would start something, and the rest of the guys would shout back. It always seemed sort of weird yet sort of fun. The Seahawks did it. Almost all the college and professional teams did it. But who would lead us?

We rocked a little, back and forth, and then Hunter's voice rang out. "What time is it?" Guys kept moving, but nobody answered. "It's butt-kicking time," he shouted. Then he did it again, only this time everybody answered.

"What time is it?"

"It's butt-kicking time!"

"Who's going kick butt?"

"We are!"

"Whose butt getting kicked?"

"Their butt getting kicked!"

"What time is it?"

"It's butt-kicking time!"

I don't know how long we chanted. Probably just a minute, but during that time every player was all in. Finally, Coach Lever yelled, "Yeah!" Practice had ended, but it felt like a beginning.

CHAPTER 14

For the next two weeks, Coach Lever stamped more of his personality onto the team. The warm-ups and drills were fast paced. When we broke into position groups, all the assistant coaches and parent volunteers had notebooks laying out exactly what they were supposed to do. I could tell Mr. Gates didn't like it, because he argued about something in the notebook, slapping at it with his hand. Coach Lever made a motion with his hands that seemed to say *You don't like it, you can leave.* Mr. Gates frowned, but he didn't leave.

Coach Lever handed out crazy prizes for everything: little toy G.I. Joes; a pass for ten minutes in a hot tub with Kate Upton. Even the wind sprints at the end of practice were almost okay. "Don't give up," Coach Lever would shout as we ran. "Don't ever give up!"

One thing I didn't like: while all the other receivers

ran a variety of pass patterns—slants, curls, down-and-outs—I ran nothing but deep stuff. That must have been in Coach Lever's notebook too. I caught a decent number of those long balls, but when you don't run anything over the middle, guys notice. "They're going to sew *Wuss* instead of *Ripley* on the back of your uniform," Colton said, grinning, and the other receivers laughed.

One day after practice, I managed to work myself over to Coach Lever. "You can send me over the middle," I told him. "Last year I backed off, but I won't this year. I'm not afraid."

He waved that off. "You've got speed, Brock, and that's a gift. I watched the film of the Bothell game. You're our vertical threat. You work on that, get that timing down. We've got Colton and Ty and a bunch of other guys for plays over the middle."

"But I want to make the tough catches too. And I can do it. I won't chicken out."

"That's good to know. And if the time comes, I'll call on you. That's a promise. Until then, keep flying downfield, all right?"

When spring football came to an end, Coach Lever called us around. "You guys can be really good. How good is up to you. Go to camps, lift weights, practice hard, and come back in August ready to rumble."

We let out a cheer and then lined up and shook hands with Coach Payne, whose eyes got teary as he said goodbye. When I turned to head for home, Mr. Gates's voice stopped me. "Hey, Brock, come back here a minute."

I jogged back. He put his arm around my shoulder and gave me a shake. "Hunter's going to be attending quarterback camps around the country in June and July, but he'll be back in Seattle in August. We'll be looking for you at Gilman Park. You'll be there, right?"

CHAPTER 15

Mr. Gupta had asked everybody on the chess team to stop by his room when school let out for summer break. Black and white balloons were tied to the corners of a table. On the table sat a chocolate cake that had been frosted to look like a chessboard. Mr. Gupta had made an animated PowerPoint presentation that had boulders jumping up and down with the words CHESS ROCKS! tilting this way while *"We will, we will rock you!"* looped through the wimpy computer speakers. The whole thing was nerdish beyond belief, but I ate a piece of goopy cake and laughed at the PowerPoint. Anya was there, which made it better, but Richie didn't show.

After about fifteen minutes, Anya got a text from her father, who was waiting in the parking lot. Once she'd left, I gobbled a final piece of cake, shook Mr. Gupta's hand, and took off.

The quickest way out of the building was through

Suicide Alley and then out a side exit. I'd avoided using that hallway—it was the older guys' last chance to muscle anyone, and the last day had a reputation for being rough. But now—fifteen minutes after the final bell—Suicide Alley seemed safe enough, and using it would save me time.

Still, before heading down it, I took a long look. I saw one person. Was it Richie? All I could see was his back, but it looked like him. He was ahead of me by thirty yards, and I was about to call out when a bunch of football guys—Hunter at the front—came spilling out of a side hallway. Had they been a minute later or a minute earlier, nothing would have happened.

But they weren't.

"Hey, Fang, what's up?" I heard one of Hunter's friends call out, pointing at Richie and then sticking out his teeth like a vampire and grinning. Richie put his head down and tried to push by them to the exit.

Colton put out his arm to stop him, and a moment later Hunter and a bunch of guys were on him. They lifted him up off the ground and carried him to the exit door. I wanted to yell out, but my throat was so tight, I could barely breathe. And I was afraid that if I tried to stop them, they'd turn on me, too.

I ducked into a classroom doorway and leaned against the wall, taking deep breaths while trying not to make a sound. But I couldn't just hide; I had to know what was happening.

I peeked out as someone pushed open the door leading to the back parking lot. At the top of the stairs was a garbage can overflowing with candy wrappers, yogurt cups, and half-eaten lunches. I watched as Hunter kicked the lid off and looked at Colton. On some invisible signal, the two of them flipped Richie over, dumping him headfirst into the garbage. Colton then tipped the can onto its side, Hunter gave it a quick, hard kick, and it rolled down the dozen steps, picking up speed as it went. The garbage can rolled across the pathway and didn't stop until it reached the grass. Hunter and Colton and the rest of them grabbed each other, laughing hard, as Richie crawled out. His hair, his face, and his shirt were covered with wet slop. In the trees, crows started cawing like mad and flying from branch to branch.

I thought Hunter and the other guys might do more, but—maybe because of the crazy way the crows were acting—that was the end. "See you next year, Fag," Hunter yelled down at him, and then the whole bunch walked away.

After taking a few deep breaths, I stepped out from my hiding place, then walked down the hallway and out into the sunlight. When I saw Richie, I pretended to be surprised. I don't know how good an acting job I did, but it didn't matter. He was working so hard to get the slimy crap off his clothes and face and out of his hair that he didn't notice me.

He pulled gunk from his neck, threw it on the ground, and then spit a few times to get something out of his mouth that was making him gag. When he finally looked up and saw me, his eyes were filled with fury. He glared for a moment, and then he pointed his finger at me. "Hunter Gates did this. But this is the last thing he's going to do to me. You're his friend, so you tell him that for me. You tell him he does one more thing and he'll pay. You tell him."

"I'm *not* his friend, Richie!" I protested.

"Yeah, you are. You'd lick his boots if he asked you. You know you would. So you tell him."

"I've never been his friend."

He wiped his hands on his pants. He looked like he was about to say more, but instead he turned and stormed off. He went about twenty feet and then turned back, pointing his finger at me as if it were a gun. "Tell him, Brock. For his own good, tell him."

After he'd vanished around a corner, I sat down on the steps and put my head in my hands. I'd been sitting there for five minutes or so when the door behind me opened. I looked back and saw Ms. Fontelle, the dance teacher, exiting the school.

She smiled. "Why so glum, chum? You're out for the summer." Then her eyes went past me and she saw the garbage can on the lawn with wrappers and soda cans tumbling out. "Did somebody get canned?"

It took me a while to answer. "Richie Fang," I finally said.

"The violinist?"

"Hunter Gates and some other guys on the football team got him."

She frowned. "Just once I'd like to get through the last day without something like this." She paused. "Is Richie okay? He wasn't hurt, was he?"

"He's okay."

Ms. Fontelle looked into the distance, staring at nothing. Finally, she turned back to me. "Look, I'm headed to Sea-Tac in two hours. Spain and Portugal. My guess is that over the summer all this will blow over. That's what almost always happens. But if this starts up again in September, you report it to Mr. Spady. And you tell him to talk to me. Okay?"

I nodded.

She smiled. "You're Troy Merrick, right? I had your sister Megan a few years ago."

"No. I'm Brock Ripley."

She gave me a puzzled look. "Well, have a good summer, Brock, and I'll see you in the fall."

PART FOUR

CHAPTER

Dog Walker. Lawn Mower. Flowerbed Weeder. Those were the jobs I came up with when I brainstormed ways to make money during the summer. I designed a flyer, made twenty copies, and posted them on telephone poles around the neighborhood. And who called first? Our next-door neighbor with her crazy beagle. "You'll love Snuffles. She's a sweet dog. If you could walk her for an hour every morning, that would be great."

I was never going to love Snuffles, but making money for taking a walk was a good deal, even if I did have to clean up poop.

Most mornings I walked Snuffles down to Gilman Park. The first few days, I tried to get her to fetch a rubber ball, but what she truly loved was garbage cans. So I'd lead her around the park, letting her sniff each trash can for a couple minutes before heading to the next one.

While she was sniffing, I'd find myself looking out

over the soccer field, thinking about Richie. I hated myself for hiding while he was being stuffed into a garbage can. I wanted to go back in time and stand up for him, even if it meant I got the same treatment.

The first few days of summer, I texted him, but he never replied. A couple of times on the weekend, I walked over to his house. Both times, his mom's car was in the same spot in the driveway, growing dirtier and dirtier. All the curtains in all the windows were drawn; the front door was tightly shut even on hot days, and an eerie silence hung over the entire place.

I knocked on the front door, but no one answered. I walked down the driveway to the shed and knocked there. No answer. Had they gone on vacation? Or had they just gone away?

It wasn't even July fourth, and I was bored. My dad was back to full-time work at the bank; my mom analyzed ridership trends for the Metro bus system, and summer was always her busiest time. I had the dog walking in the morning and a couple of weeding jobs had come through, but nothing steady.

The weight room at school was open. So after I walked the beagle, I lifted weights and ran intervals at Crown Hill, but that still left my afternoons empty. Coach Lever wanted us to sign up for football camps. That's what Hunter and Colton and most guys would be doing.

I didn't want to fall behind, so I went online and searched. There were some local camps, and they weren't too expensive, but all of them were in Bellevue or Woodinville or Shoreline. How would I get to them? I didn't want to ask my dad to do extra driving, and my mom was way too busy. Then I remembered that in August I'd be working out with Hunter and his father. That would have to be my camp.

CHAPTER 2

Hey, isn't this your friend?"

It was a Saturday morning in mid-July. My dad was sitting at the kitchen table reading the *Westside Weekly*, a local newspaper that was packed with ads. His finger was tapping on a short article with the headline CROWN HILL STUDENT TAKES FIRST.

He slid the paper over to me and I read the article, my mouth breaking into a smile. "Yeah, that's Richie. He built an eco-friendly model of our school, everything green. Solar panels and daylighted creeks and natural light in the classrooms—stuff like that. He added a new wing powered entirely by renewable energy. His model is incredible—I thought he was going to win. Now he gets to go to a national competition."

"You should go see him," my dad said. "He seemed like a good kid, even if he did act crazy at the Lakeside game."

"I've been a couple times, but he hasn't been around."

"Probably they were down in Portland. Go over to his house and congratulate him."

I went that afternoon. There was a beat-up white car in front of the house, and I heard salsa music coming from the front room. I walked around to the back and saw that the shed door was wide open. "Richie," I called out. "You there?" He came out, a broad smile on his face that reminded me of the old Richie. "Congrats," I told him. "I knew you'd win."

He tried to shrug it off. "It was no big deal. The big deal is Pittsburgh in December. There's scholarship money for that one, and they display the winning model at this great museum that used to be a mattress factory."

"Come on. You won. Be happy."

His smiled got even broader. "All right. I'm happy."

We bumped fists, and I peered over his shoulder. "Are you still working on it?"

"Repairs. My dad drove it to Portland in a rented van. I put foam all around it, but it still got banged up pretty good."

"You feel like a break? We could go to Gilman and kick a soccer ball around."

He checked the time on his cell phone. "Okay, but I've got to be back in an hour."

* * *

We didn't talk much, just booted the soccer ball back and forth, running a little this way and that, stopping the ball with our chests or our feet, heading a ball now and then, breaking a sweat and feeling the right amount of tired.

After about forty minutes, we took a long drink at the fountain and then sat down under the maple trees that lined the perimeter of the park.

The day was warm, but not hot. Richie lay back on the grass, looking at the sky, so I did the same. For a while, neither of us spoke. But I knew what he was thinking about.

"How's your mom?" I asked.

"Not good. She's talking about hospice."

"What's that?"

"It's when you give up. The doctors don't try to cure you; they just make sure nothing hurts. She doesn't want any more chemotherapy. My dad is totally opposed. 'Fight! Fight! Fight!' he says. He's like a football coach."

I stared up at the clouds, big puffy things floating across the sky. I thought of how my dad had said that for someone who was unlucky, he was lucky, and I knew he was right.

Richie sat up and spun the soccer ball on his finger. "My dad is on the phone with people in Nanjing all the time. He's got a job lined up. If my mom dies, we'll be gone in a month, maybe sooner."

The thought just sat there for a while. "Would it be that bad?" I asked. "You lived there before, right?"

"We left when I was five. My Mandarin sucks. I can understand it okay, but I can't read much. And all I remember about Nanjing is that the air sometimes got so polluted, I had to wear a mask when I went outside."

CHAPTER 3

Suddenly, my days were full. In the morning, I walked Snuffles, lifted weights at Crown Hill High, ran the track, and then ate lunch. If I didn't have a weeding job, I'd make it to Richie's house most days around one. I'd walk down the driveway and stick my head in the shed. He'd be inside, working on his project even though there wasn't much that needed doing.

It turned out that the beat-up white car belonged to a home health worker who stayed with his mom for two hours every afternoon. "She's not a nurse," Richie explained. "She comes in, sits in the front room, watches TV, and then, after a couple of hours, leaves. But my dad doesn't want my mom to be alone, and he doesn't want me to spend all day at the house. So for two hours every afternoon, I'm free."

We spent the time at Gilman Park. We didn't talk

about his mother again, or my father or China or Hunter Gates or Crown Hill High. We just kicked the soccer ball around.

I'd be lying if I said I didn't notice when August neared. Mr. Gates had said that he and Hunter would be back at Gilman Park, and that meant they'd be expecting me to run pass routes for him.

Most of the time when I thought about Hunter, I just hated the guy. He was such a jerk—to Richie, to Suzanne Friend, and no doubt to a bunch of other kids. The Hunter Gates who strutted around like he was king of the world—I wanted nothing to do with him, ever.

But there was that other Hunter Gates—the Hunter with the great arm, the Hunter who knew where I'd be on the field before I did. When I caught passes thrown by *that* Hunter Gates, it was as if I were an eagle gliding over Puget Sound. Nothing else in the world felt that way.

On the last day of July, I downloaded the permission slip for football and took it to my parents. My mom repeated her condition about concussions, I agreed, and she signed. "Good luck," my dad said, and then he signed too.

The next afternoon, as Richie and I kicked the soccer ball back and forth, I kept expecting to see Hunter and his father pile out of their car and take the field. What would

I do then? How could I explain to Richie that I needed to work out with Hunter?

When they didn't show, I was relieved. But when they didn't show the next day, or the next, I got worried. What, exactly, had Mr. Gates said? August first? Or just August? I couldn't remember.

As the days rolled by, I grew more nervous. What if Hunter wasn't coming at all? Colton and the other receivers had gone to football camps. They'd been practicing with top-notch coaches while I'd been kicking a soccer ball around. I needed to catch a football, to catch lots of footballs, to get my feel back before tryouts. Since my dad couldn't throw passes to me, and it didn't look like Hunter was going to show, who could?

It had to be Richie.

The next day, I brought my football. Richie looked at it as if it were a huge dog turd. "What's that for?"

I explained.

He scowled. "I don't get why you go out for football."

"I'm fast and I can catch. Hauling in a long touchdown pass—it's even better than scoring a goal."

His eyebrows went up. "And how would you know what scoring a goal feels like?"

"Very funny, Richie."

He shrugged. "All right. I'll throw to you, but I'm telling you right now I'm going to suck."

He was right. His hands were so small, he could

barely grip the football. He also had a weird arm motion, almost sidearm. After five throws, we both knew it wasn't working.

"I told you," he said.

"How about you kick some?"

"What good will that do?"

"It'll give me practice watching the ball into my hands. Punts are hard to catch." He looked doubtful. "Really," I insisted. "It'll help."

I didn't know if it would. And when Richie's first kick was a shank that traveled five yards forward and about thirty yards to the right, I was even less certain.

"Let me throw it to you," he said after I'd run the ball down and tossed it back to him. "I don't know how to kick one of these."

"Kick it a few more times," I called back. "It's not all that different from kicking a soccer ball."

"It's completely different," he said, but on his third try he made solid contact with the ball, sailing one way over my head. And after that, kick after kick was high and deep. Okay, he missed some—even great kickers miss some—but not many.

It was a windy day, so the ball was blowing around, forcing me to concentrate. Catching kicks wasn't like running patterns for Hunter, but it was something.

That night, when I was on Minecraft with some guy in South Africa, I replayed Richie's kicks in my mind. The ball came off his foot, traveled about ten yards or so like anybody else's, and then seemed to rocket through the air as if it had afterburners. I tried to figure out how far his punts had gone. There were no yard markers at Gilman, but it seemed like they went at least thirty-five yards, and maybe forty or forty-five.

Whenever I'd thought about Richie back at school walking the hallways, I'd get so sick to my stomach that I'd start burping this acid stuff that tasted like vomit. Hunter and those guys would go after him again, just like they'd gone after Jerry Jumper. They never backed off once they'd started.

Unless.

CHAPTER 4

The next day, as we walked to Gilman, I put my idea to him.

His eyes went wide. "Me, the kicker for the football team? You're joking, right?"

"Why not give it a try? I know you don't want to go home right after school. Football would give you something to do. Besides, you'd be good."

He shook his head. "Hunter Gates doesn't want me on his team. And I don't want to be on his team."

"It's not *his* team, and he *will* want you on it. You kick the ball ten yards farther than anybody we've got, and your kicks are higher, which makes them easy for the punt team to cover. You'll be first string—I guarantee it. You'll be good at field goals too. They're closer to soccer kicks, and you can win games kicking field goals. Just picture it, Richie. It's the last play. Everybody is up on both sides, screaming their lungs out, and you split the uprights with a field goal to win the game. The stadium goes berserk. You're the hero, and your picture is in the paper and your kick is on YouTube."

The chance to be a star pulled him. I could see it in his eyes. He didn't say yes, but he didn't say no, either. Once we reached the park, we didn't spend even a minute with soccer. It was all punting. Richie must have been concentrating more, because he'd didn't have a single kick go off the side of his foot. When he was tired of punting, I held for him and he tried placekicking. Most of his attempts were low line drives that could get blocked, but coaching and practice would fix that.

"I've got a joke for you," he said as we headed off the field. "Ready?"

"Go ahead. I'm ready."

"Okay. Harry Potter, the GEICO gecko, and Taylor Swift walk into a bar. The bartender looks at them and says, 'What is this? A joke?'"

He told a couple more that were slightly funny, and I told a couple that weren't funny at all. After that, we walked in silence until we reached his house. "So what do you say?" I asked. "Will you try out?"

He took the football from me and squeezed it a couple of times. "You really think I can do this?"

"All the NFL kickers were soccer players first. You kick a soccer ball better than anyone in the school. You know you do. It'll be the same with a football, once you practice."

A little smile crept across his face. "Walking down the center of the hallways at Crown Hill as a football star—that feels perfect, like living out an O. Henry story." He paused. "Okay, I'll do it."

I high-fived him and then gave him a chest-high fist-bump. For a moment, everything was perfect.

Once everything ended, people told me that what happened wasn't my fault, and I guess it wasn't. But I was the one who talked Richie into trying out for the team. That's on me.

CHAPTER

The night before tryouts, I played chess with my dad. I was thinking about football more than the pieces, so he checkmated me in fifteen moves. "Another game?" he said automatically.

I was about to say no—automatically—and head upstairs, but something made me look into his face, to really look. He was pale and his skin sagged, but it was the hurt in his eyes that froze me.

I'd let him down with my shoddy effort, not just in that game, but in most of our chess games. He could have been angry. You hear about sick people who lash out, but he wasn't that way, and I couldn't see him ever becoming that way. "I sucked in that one," I said. "I'll give you a better game this time."

He smiled, surprised, and he rubbed his hands together in anticipation. "I'll take black again."

I concentrated on every move, and it was forty minutes before I could see there was no way to keep him from promoting a pawn.

"Good game," I said, reaching across the board to shake his hand.

"It was, Brock. Thanks."

The next morning, Richie and I walked to tryouts together. We reached the field early, but other guys were already milling around. I spotted Hunter on the far side of the field, tossing a football to Colton.

Coach Lever was in the middle of the field, up on a little platform. He sounded a bullhorn and motioned for all of us to gather around him.

"Here we go," I said to Richie as we headed toward the platform.

Colton saw Richie first. He nudged Hunter and pointed, and then their faces broke into big grins. Hunter looked to the side and called out to somebody I couldn't see. "Look who's trying out."

More faces turned toward us; more fingers pointed; more guys gaped. "Look, Fag's here!" somebody called out.

Coach Lever heard. "Knock that off," he shouted, striding toward the group. It was the first time I'd seen him angry. Hunter and the guys in his posse fell silent.

Ten minutes later, we were doing warm-up drills. My eyes went to the freshmen kids. Some acted tough, but they were all scared. They were me a year ago.

Coach Lever made pushups, jumping jacks, and stretches both harder and more fun with his loud music and his crazy prizes. For a few minutes at the end, we actually played *Mother May I?*

Once we were loose, the assistant coaches and the adult volunteers pinned numbers to our shirts and timed us in the forty-yard dash. After that, we broke into position groups, Coach Lever shouting out where we were to go. I was directed to follow Mr. Gates to the north end zone. I took a step, but then I saw Richie, standing by himself, looking lost. Was there a parent or coach in charge of kicking? I grabbed him by the arm and led him to Coach Lever.

"Coach," I said, talking really fast so he wouldn't interrupt, "this is Richie Fang. He doesn't really play football, but he can kick."

Coach Lever looked Richie up and down.

"How far can you punt it?"

Richie shrugged.

"Fifty yards," I said, jumping in. "With good hang time."

"Fifty yards? And with hang time?" Coach Lever pulled on one of his diamond earrings and smiled. "Shouldn't he be trying out for the Seahawks?"

"Really," I insisted. "Not all the time, but sometimes. And we've got no kicker, right?"

He considered. "All right, we'll give him a look." He turned to Richie. "Tell me your name again."

Richie told him.

Coach Lever turned to one of the parent volunteers. "Mr. Breuner, I'd like you to take Richie over to the baseball field and have him punt for you." He turned back to Richie. "Can you placekick?"

"Sure."

Lever turned back to the parent. "And have him kick from a tee, too."

CHAPTER

I raced down the field to catch up with the receivers and quarterbacks. Mr. Gates was holding the set of directions he'd gotten from Coach Lever. I got in the receivers' line and did the drills. At first, I was afraid I'd be miles behind Colton, but my morning workouts at the track had kept up my speed and endurance, and my hands still drew the ball in like a vacuum cleaner sucks up dirt.

When I wasn't running pass routes, I peeked at Richie. He was positioned just behind home plate, and Mr. Breuner was standing behind second base. Richie would take a step forward and boot the ball. The kicks looked good, but it was hard to tell how far they were going.

Then, for the first time in my life, I used some of the geometry I'd learned. It was ninety feet from home to first and another ninety from first to second. Home to second was the hypotenuse of a triangle. That made it around forty yards. All of Richie's kicks were past second base. That meant over forty yards in the air, and they all soared high—not good enough for the Seahawks, but plenty good for high school.

I ran a deep post pattern, caught the pass, and jogged back to the back of the line. The next time I looked over, Coach Lever was standing with Mr. Breuner. Hunter threw a pass to one of the freshmen. I moved forward in the line, my eyes still sneaking peeks at Richie. I watched him kick a ball high and deep. Coach Lever walked over and put his hand up, and Richie high-fived him.

"Brock, wake up!" Mr. Gates screamed at me. "Deep out. Go."

I ran the pattern, caught the ball, and trotted back. Aiden stepped into the QB spot; Hunter stepped aside to rest his arm. As I worked up the line, I saw Hunter look over at the baseball field to watch Richie kick.

The receiving drills ended, and then came agility, strength, and quickness drills—all done with hard rock blasting across the field, but all done with precision. At the end came the gassers—a series of wind sprints. Whenever I thought I couldn't do another one, some old Credence or Stones song would come rolling across the grass, and I'd run again.

When the bullhorn sounded, everyone was drenched in sweat. "Good work, men," Coach Lever called out. "Really good work. See you tomorrow."

Richie and I headed off the field. We were just about

down the steps when I heard Colton's voice behind us. "What are you doing here, Fag?"

"Just keep walking," I whispered.

Richie stopped. "I'm not running, Brock."

He turned and faced Colton and Hunter and the others standing with them.

"You talking to me?" Richie said with a New York gangster accent. Richie was mocking Colton, but Colton didn't get it.

"Yeah, I'm talking to you," Colton said. "Unless there's another Fang-Fag around."

"Shut up, Sparks," Hunter snapped.

Colton looked at Hunter, stunned. "What?"

"I said shut up."

Colton motioned toward Richie. "You want him on the team?"

Hunter didn't answer.

"Get a clue, Colton," I said. "Richie can kick. Nobody else can. So back off."

Hunter glared at Richie. "Just don't screw up, Fang. Understand? Nothing like how the soccer season ended. No crap like that."

Richie glared right back. "You're telling *me* not to screw up? That's a good joke. How many interceptions did you throw last year, Gates? Was it fifteen or sixteen? Or did you lose count?"

Hunter's hands balled into fists. He looked as if he

wanted to spring down the stairs and pound Richie into the earth. Then his hands relaxed. He walked down the stairway, brushed past us, and headed off the field, the other guys trailing behind him.

When they were fifty yards ahead, I turned to Richie. He was smiling, and I realized I was grinning too.

"How did you know about his interceptions?" I asked.

"It's in the newspaper archives. I know all his numbers. He's not that good."

I shook my head. "Actually, he's great. He throws tight spirals. He's tough as nails. He understands the game. He just needs a receiver who can get deep and a kicker who can flip field position for him."

Richie snorted. "So you and me are going to help him snag a scholarship to Ohio State? Is that what you're saying?"

I punched him lightly on the shoulder. "Remember, we'll be stars too."

CHAPTER 7

Nobody called out "Fag" as Richie walked across the field before tryouts the next day. Hunter had put out the word—leave Richie alone.

We did the warm-up drills together, but after that Richie worked with Mr. Breuner, while I was with Mr. Gates. Bob Rohas, the long snapper, spent time practicing with Richie. Some days, Breuner brought guys over to simulate a rush. Richie wasn't flustered; he caught the ball and kicked it no matter what was going on around him.

The year before, if you screwed up, you heard about it from the coaches. Now, because of Coach Lever, it was all about the *next time*. "Next time, keep your head up." "Next time, don't let the pass get into your body." "Next time, make the cut sharper." With stuff that couldn't be fixed right away, Lever still stayed positive. "Put in the effort and you'll get there. The way we practice is the way we'll play."

"It's because of the Seahawks," my dad said at dinner. "Their coaches are always pumping their guys up, and the Hawks are winning, so your coaches are trying it too."

One thing we didn't do at practice was tackle one another. Instead, the coaches worked us on sleds and tackling dummies, teaching both how to deliver a hit and how to take one without getting a concussion.

The lack of contact bothered me. I was a deep threat, a game breaker, and a lock to make the team. But when you've got the tag of *wuss* hanging over your head, you want to get rid of it. The quickest way to prove I wasn't gutless would be to take a big hit from a safety or a linebacker, pop up, toss the ball to a referee, and trot back to the huddle as if nothing had ever happened. But how could I do that if I never got the chance?

The night before the big scrimmage, I lay on my bed and relived the humiliations of the year before. The hits, the drops, the short arms, the vomiting. After I'd played that horror movie in my head three or four times, I walked down the hall to the bathroom and stared at myself in the mirror. I was bigger, taller, and stronger—no doubt about it. I told myself I was ready, that I could take a hit and hang on to the ball, that this year was going to be different. Then I looked again and saw the same scared kid as before.

CHAPTER 8

As we neared the field on the last day of tryouts, Richie started whistling. "Aren't you even a little nervous?" I asked.

"Nope. Free, like my birds in Nanjing. Full leg extension, relaxed muscles, let it go. I do that and the ball soars high and deep. If I worry, my muscles get tight and the ball goes short and sideways, so I can't worry. Did you ever see a worried bird?"

"But you didn't have any birds. You made that all up."

He smiled. "Sure, I had birds. Twenty-three of them, and they flew around my room pooping on my head."

Coach Lever had posted the depth chart on a fence near midfield. I was the number four receiver on the Red Team—Hunter's team. My spirits sank—I thought I'd be no lower than three, and maybe number two.

I started the game on the bench, watching—my body aching for action—as Hunter led the Red team down the field, mixing runs and passes, chewing up yards. I was sure he was going to lead the team in for a score, but on second-and-four on the Black twenty-yard line he fumbled the snap and lost three yards. "Get in there," Coach Lever shouted at me. "Eighty-eight down and out."

I pulled on my helmet and raced onto the field. I was so nervous that when I repeated the play call, my voice squeaked like a girl's. Nobody noticed. "Everybody got that?" Hunter yelled. "Okay. On two."

The guys broke the huddle.

"Hut! Hut!"

I took off, driving downfield five yards. Then I pivoted, breaking toward the sideline. The pass was supposed to arrive when I was five yards from the sideline, and Hunter was perfect with the delivery. I hauled the pass in and looked upfield—open space. If I turned, I'd gain five more yards, maybe more, before the safety hit me. I wanted to turn; I wanted to take that hit, to scratch out the extra yards; but—and here's where I don't understand myself—I didn't take on the safety. Instead, I ran, untouched, out of bounds. It was the decision my mother would have wanted me to make.

Had Coach Lever noticed? Had Hunter? Had anyone?

I flipped the ball to the ref and trotted back to the sidelines.

Coach Lever clapped. "Good catch."

I stayed on the bench. Colton Sparks and Ty Erdman, our slot receiver, were on the field ninety percent of the time. Every once in a while, Coach Lever would send me out. Every time, I ran deep patterns or out patterns, pulling a safety and a cornerback with me. Each time, I hoped to see a pass spiraling toward me, but Hunter kept firing short bullets to Colton and Ty.

As the game wore on, Coach Lever started calling running plays for Skeeter Washington, a muscular black kid who'd transferred from Texas. He was like a bowling ball, breaking tackles and piling up yardage.

Then, right when I was sure I wouldn't even get on the field again, Lever slapped me on the shoulder. "Eighty-eight vertical in," he said.

The down was second-and-six. The safeties had been pinching in to stop Skeeter. I relayed the call to Hunter, who had to have been sick of running plays and short passes. "You heard him," Hunter said to the guys huddling around him. "On one."

I'd just reached my spot way out to the left when I heard *"Rocket!"* I exploded off the line, broke past the cornerback, and cut to the middle of the field. When I looked back, the ball was already in the air. It dropped from the sky like a soft Seattle rain. I hauled it in without breaking stride, and then I was gone.

Touchdown!

My teammates jumped up and down; Hunter high-fived me; Coach Lever did a Tiger Woods fist pump.

That was it for me. Two catches: one for a first down and the other for a touchdown. I wanted to believe that I'd played a great football game, and in a way I had. But I hadn't tackled anybody: I hadn't even hit the ground. The guys around me were dirty and bruised, their pants ripped, their elbows bleeding. I was embarrassed by my spotless uniform.

As I gathered my stuff, Colton came over to me, and I knew what was coming. "You wearing a bra yet?" he asked, his voice soft but his mean smile right up in my face.

I felt my face flush.

"You know why Lever has no plays for you over the middle? You know why you're not on any special teams? It's because you're a girl, Ripley. Coach Lever knows it; every guy on the team knows it. Your gay lover over there"—he nodded toward Richie—"has bigger stones than you, and the whole school has seen how tiny his are."

Colton waited a beat, daring me to take a swing at him. When I didn't, he snorted and walked away. My hands were shaking so much that I struggled to zip shut my duffle bag. Why hadn't I taken a shot at him?

"What was that about?" Richie asked when he came over.

"Nothing. Just Colton being his normal jerk self."

CHAPTER 9

When I opened my front door around two that afternoon, the house was empty. I could have eaten or showered or turned on ESPN or my laptop. Instead, I went to my room, flicked off the light, pulled down the shades, and lay on the bed in the near dark, still feeling the sting of Colton Sparks's words.

I stayed up there in the dark until my mother came home. Then I flicked on the light and pretended that I'd spent the afternoon playing video games.

At dinner, my dad asked about the scrimmage. I described my two catches.

"That's great. Sounds like you were the star receiver."

"I wouldn't say that. Colton Sparks had at least six catches, and Ty Erdman caught a bunch too."

I skipped chess that evening. I told my dad I was too tired to give him a decent game but that I'd play him twice the next night. Upstairs, I wasted time reading everything on the CBS Sports website and then did the same on ESPN's.

When I'd exhausted the Internet, I shut the laptop and thought about the tryout. Only this time around, I thought about the team's prospects and not my own game. I was sick of thinking about my own game.

Richie would make the kicking game better. Skeeter Washington was a load; he'd do the same for the running game. Hunter was throwing the ball great—all his summer quarterback camps had paid off. I hated to admit it, but Colton Sparks was catching the ball better too. And then there was Coach Lever. He had been an assistant coach at some great football dynasty in Georgia. He was constantly making improvements in technique, in plays, in communication, in everything. He expected to win, and the team had sucked up confidence from him.

Saturday afternoon, I headed over to Richie's house. He was in the shed, as usual, making invisible improvements to the wing he'd added to his eco-school. As he worked, I tried to get him talking about the football team and about our chances in the upcoming season.

He should have been pumped. He'd done the punting for both the Red and the Black teams, probably booting half a dozen punts in all. His worst punt went at least thirty-five yards in the air; the best probably went fifty. He hadn't fumbled a snap; he hadn't shanked a kick off the side of his foot. And he was solid as a placekicker, too. He made four extra points, and though he missed a field goal from thirty-five he made a field goal from twenty-five on the last play of the scrimmage. "You should read up on the game," I told him. "I bet if you read about all the great kickers, you'd like football more."

"That's a good idea," he answered, his head down. His model had his full attention; my football talk was background noise.

Finally, he stretched his arms above his head, groaned a little, and then turned and took something off a shelf behind him. "Look at this," he said unrolling a poster. It was for the Pittsburgh contest. In the center was a photo of a scale model of a skyscraper. "That's last year's winning project."

I looked it over, taking my time. "It's cool, but yours is just as good."

He nodded. "I think so too. Actually, I think mine's better. There's more to mine, with the daylighted creek, the water system, the solar panels, the natural light, and the new wing. I just wish the contest were this week."

"What's the hurry? December's better. By then, you'll probably have won some violin competition, a math contest, and a chess tournament and kicked a bunch of game-winning field goals. You'll need some new excitement."

He laughed, but then the smile disappeared. "I want my mom to see me win. She wanted to be an architect, but her parents pushed her into science. This is for her."

CHAPTER 10

"Is it true?"

Those were Anya's first words to me on the opening day of school. We'd run into each other on the way to Mr. Gupta's room at lunch. I'd said hello, but instead of answering she'd grabbed me by the arm and pulled me over to a semiquiet spot.

"Is what true?" I asked.

"That you've got Richie playing on the football team?"

I nodded. "What's so bad about that?"

"Are you out of your mind? Hunter Gates. Colton Sparks. And that's just for starters."

"No, Anya, you don't get it. They've backed off. They'll leave Richie alone now. He's part of the team."

"Oh, right, Brock. Hunter Gates is going to be looking out for Richie, his Asian bro. He'll be looking out for him all right—so that he can throw him in a dumpster."

My face reddened. She couldn't have known what had happened to Richie on the last day of school. He wouldn't have told anyone, and I was the only one who'd seen.

I pulled myself together. "Anya, Richie is not just *on* the football team. He's a big part of the football team. He's better at kicking than anybody on the team, and the kicking game matters. Hunter needs to make a name for himself, and the only way to do that is to win. Richie can help win games, so Hunter has to leave Richie alone."

She didn't answer, and as the seconds passed her face softened. "I hope you know what you're doing," she said at last.

"Trust me. I do."

We walked down the hallway together. Twenty feet from Gupta's room, we heard Richie's voice, full of life. And when we stepped inside, we saw him at the center table, sitting across a chessboard from Mr. Gupta. He gave me a wave, and he gave Anya his best smile.

"I've got a joke for you, Anya," he shouted, tipping his chair back. "You listening?"

"Do I have a choice?"

"An old guy was in the park playing chess with his dog, a Jack Russell terrier. A woman came by and said, 'I'd heard those were smart dogs, but I had no idea they were smart enough to play chess.'

"'Ah, he's not so smart,' the old guy answered as he put the chess pieces away. 'I beat him two out of three.'"

CHAPTER 11

We opened the football season against the Franklin Quakers. I'd read up on them in the *Seattle Times.* They'd lost every single game the year before, and their head coach had quit once the season ended. The new coach said that he was building for the future. That was code for *This year's team sucks.*

Still, everybody was nervous before the opening kickoff. First games are like that. The band is playing, and most of the school is there. The weather is still warm; the sky is light.

Franklin won the coin toss and took the ball first. They made a couple of first downs, but then a holding penalty forced them to punt. I stayed along the sideline and watched Hunter lead the team downfield, mixing handoffs to Skeeter Washington with passes to Colton and Ty. We drove to the seven-yard line, but then came a penalty and a botched handoff. On third down from the sixteen, I got my first action. I ran a deep post, but Franklin double-teamed me with a strong safety, so Hunter hit Colton with a short pass over the middle good for nine yards. On fourth down, Coach Lever sent Richie out for a field goal.

It was the first quarter of the first game, but it was an important moment. If your kicker can't hit a short field goal against a team that sucks, then there's no way a coach will trust him in the fourth quarter of a big game. Richie—cool as ice—split the uprights. A siren went off; the band played the fight song; the cheer team ran up and down the sidelines.

As Richie came off the field, the special team guys slapped his helmet and whacked his shoulder pads. On the sidelines, Coach Lever gave him a high-five. Richie pulled his helmet off, grinned at me, and then realized he needed to pull it right back on again for the kickoff.

The score was still 3–0 when we got the ball back. The second drive was also a steady diet of short passes and runs. Eight yards, six yards, seven yards. I got on the field for a couple of plays, both times running deep patterns that cleared the underneath for Colton. Then with third-and-inches at their twenty-five, Coach Lever called another play for me.

The route was double eighty-eight in. Hunter's voice was tense as he called it. A bunch of short passes weren't going to be enough to catch the eye of a bigtime college coach—he needed some highlight-reel completions.

As I split out wide, the safety crept in, anticipating a run. That meant single coverage. The play called for me to drive forward about five yards, pretend to curl back, but then break long down the sideline. Since I had to make two moves, the play would take time to develop. The blocking had to be great.

And it was. The cornerback bit on my first move, so on the second move I streaked down the sideline, open by five yards. Hunter laid the ball out for me. It should have been an easy catch, but I lost it in the low sky for a second. When I picked it up again, the ball was right on me. I didn't catch it with my hands; instead, the ball bounced between my hands and my shoulder pads. Somehow I clutched it to my chest with my forearms, and then I ran like crazy for the goal line.

The strong safety had an angle, but I crossed into the end zone just before he reached me, so he pulled up. Seconds later, my teammates were surrounding me, including Hunter. They leaped on me, knocking me down, and then they pulled me up and slapped my helmet. We ran back to the bench while the siren blared, the band played, and our fans roared. Richie kicked the extra point, making the score 10–0. Two minutes later, I was still breathing fast from the excitement.

I didn't do anything else that game, but the rest of the offense rolled. Hunter and Skeeter ran the read-option in the second half, biting off huge chunks of yardage on nearly every play. Hunter mixed in underneath passes to Colton and the tight ends, piling up yards and keeping his completion rate high. The score was 38–0 starting the fourth quarter; the mercy rule kicked in, and that was the score when the game ended.

In the locker room afterward, Coach Lever told us how great the offense and defense had played. When he finished, one of the linemen jumped onto a bench and waved a flag around. "All the way to the T-Dome!" he screamed, and a roar went up.

When the team bus was a mile from school, Richie gave me a little poke in the ribs. "What was that stuff about the T-Dome?" he asked.

"That's where the state semifinals and finals are played."

"Do we have a chance to get there?"

I lowered my voice so that only he could hear. "I don't think so. But sixteen teams make the playoffs, and we could do that. We've got an easy schedule early on, but our last three games are really tough. Bellevue, Blanchet, and O'Dea are all powerhouse teams."

Richie thought for a second. "I bet the title game is

on TV. If I kicked the winning field goal, everybody in the state would see it, wouldn't they?"

That was pure Richie—he'd played one football game in his life, and he already had his eyes on the biggest stage.

CHAPTER 12

The rap music that next week was louder, and the work was harder. Agility drills, strength drills, gassers, playbook study, route tightening, tackling form, gassers, more drills, more plays, more gassers. Mr. Gates supervised the receivers and the quarterbacks, but Coach Lever came around more and more. "Make that cut sharper." "Sell your move." "You can run faster than that." And, his favorite: "You win the game at practice."

On Thursday, a guy wearing a Sacramento State Hornets sweatshirt was standing along the sidelines, his eyes on Hunter. When practice ended, Coach Lever asked both Colton and me to stick around. With the Sacramento State guy watching, the two of us took turns running patterns for Hunter: Colton taking the short routes, me going long. Hunter was so nervous that his first four passes sailed high, but then his nerves settled, and ball after ball came right on the numbers.

I caught six balls, each throw about twenty yards downfield. By then I was sucking wind, so I didn't reach the seventh even though it was actually a perfect pass. "That's it, Brock," Coach Lever called out. "You can go home now." When I left, Hunter was still throwing short stuff to Colton.

That night, I logged on to Recruits.com. Hunter was back on the list at number ninety-three. The comment next to his name read *Solid opener, accurate long and short, no INTs, a sleeper.*

I got to school early the next morning, so I headed to the library, hoping to run into Anya. She was there, her math book open and her fingers punching data into her graphing calculator. Richie was at a circular table on the other side of the library, playing video games with some guys. I was going to leave Anya alone and join them, but she smiled when she saw me.

"You don't have to study?" I asked.

She put down her calculator. "This isn't due until Friday."

I dropped my backpack on the floor and sat next to her. Just then, Richie and his entire group broke into loud laughter and started pounding on the table. Mr. Tracy, the librarian, rushed over, motioning with his hands that they needed to quiet down. Richie put a finger to his lips and shushed everybody, but his *shush* was as loud as the laughter.

Anya motioned with her head toward him. "My dad called his dad. His mother is going into hospice care."

"He told me she might," I said.

She paused. "Has he told you about moving back to China?"

"Yeah."

"He'll hate that. I speak better Mandarin than he does, and I'm just okay. I don't think he can read or write very much at all. The whole thing makes me sad. Even him acting so happy makes me sad."

I glanced at Richie again. His hands were pounding on the keyboard, and he was almost jumping up and down in his seat. In a way, it seemed strange that he could be so hyper, but maybe that's how he kept himself from thinking about his mom.

As Anya started to gather up her stuff for her class, an idea came to me. "Why don't you come to the Ingraham game? Richie would like it. Afterward, we could all go to El Camion to eat. I think they've got karaoke there. Richie told me he's really good at the 'Monster Mash.'"

CHAPTER 15

The Ingraham game was at Seattle Center under the lights. As we ran onto the field, I spotted Anya and a bunch of other chess club kids up in the stands. She waved. I didn't wave back, but Richie did—waving both hands above his head like one of the workers on an airport tarmac. "Don't do that," I whispered to him. "Coach Lever won't like you to look into the stands."

"Why?

"He just won't."

Ingraham was better than Franklin. We didn't rip off huge chunks of yardage on the running plays, but we did move the ball down the field. On our second drive, with third and goal from the six, Hunter made such a good fake to Skeeter that I didn't know he still had the ball until he was running into the end zone, hands raised above his head.

Ingraham moved the ball to midfield on their next possession, but then our defense forced a punt. The ball took a good bounce for them, pinning us way back on our own five-yard line.

Coach Lever slapped me on the helmet. "Vertical out eighty-eight," he yelled. When I relayed the play call to Hunter, he kneeled and gave the play to the team. "On one," he said.

A few seconds later, I was off. Hunter rolled to his right and then launched a long pass down the sideline.

The Ingraham cornerback was a couple of steps behind me. The ball was mine to catch, but the wind was playing tricks with the ball. I made a little slant to the outside, trying to judge the point where the ball and my hands would meet.

Then another gust of wind came. The ball fluttered, changed trajectory. I tried to adjust my speed, but I ended up having to reach back and over, only getting one hand on the ball and then watching it bounce wildly down the sideline and out of bounds. I came off the field, dejected. "Next time," Coach Lever said to me, clapping his hands. "Next time."

I was walking down the sideline to be by myself when I heard a roar from our side. I looked up and saw Hunter streaking down the field, with Ingraham players trying to chase him down. Hunter cut back at the fifty and then made a stutter-step move at the thirty. He was inside the twenty before he was finally pushed out of bounds. Two plays later, Skeeter scored. Richie kicked his second extra point, and the score was 14–0 at the half.

I sat on the bench watching Colton and Ty make catches over the middle as Hunter led the team on another long drive in the third quarter, pushing our lead to 21–0 heading into the fourth quarter.

My uniform was still spotless when I got my last chance midway through the fourth quarter. With a third-and-one, Ingraham crowded the line, expecting Skeeter or Hunter to run for the first down. Instead, Lever called for play action. I did a stop-and-go down the sideline. I was wide open, but with the wind swirling more than ever, Hunter threw a low bullet. I waited instead of working back to the ball, and the safety cut in front and broke up the pass. I didn't step on the field again.

But Richie did. The score was 21–6 with under a minute left. We had a fourth-and-one on Ingraham's twenty-three-yard line. I figured Skeeter would pound it up the middle. Even if he didn't make a first down, the game was ours.

Instead, Coach Lever sent Richie out to try a forty-yard field goal. I didn't get it. We didn't need the points—it almost seemed like running up the score. But then I figured it out. Lever wanted to give Richie a shot at a long field goal in tough conditions when it *didn't* matter.

If he could make it, he'd have more confidence when he was facing a kick that *did.*

The snap wasn't that good, so Richie didn't get all of his foot into the kick. The ball wobbled in the air, and it had a little hook to it. I leaned forward, holding my breath. Had it crawled over the crossbar, or was it short? I couldn't tell. Then the officials stepped forward and raised their arms.

Good!

On the field, guys surrounded Richie, patting him on the back, slapping his helmet, and bouncing off the field with him.

Twenty minutes later, we were taking the bus back to the school parking lot. Hunter was way up front, talking to Coach Lever. He'd had another great game, running for over one hundred yards, passing for two hundred. Everyone around me—including Richie—was in that victory glow. So what if I hadn't contributed to the win. Other guys on the team hadn't done much, and they were laughing. I decided to forget about my own game and enjoy the ride.

When we got off the bus, Anya and a handful of kids from the chess club were waiting for us. We walked to El Camion on Fifteenth and split a couple of orders of nachos.

As we ate, we talked a little about the game, but then Heather, one of the new girls in the club, mentioned what Allishya Soderheim had worn to school that day. "Did you see how low cut her sweater was? And that push-up bra?"

Richie opened his eyes in a fake innocence. "I didn't see anything."

"You guys wish we all dressed like that," Anya said, half smiling and half scowling.

"Guys wish we had boobs like that," Heather said, a similar half scowl, half smile, on her face. Then she looked around at the other girls at the table. "Actually, we wish we had boobs like that."

Everybody laughed. I didn't say anything, but I didn't wish that, at least not for Anya.

CHAPTER 14

When I went downstairs the next morning, my dad was sitting at the kitchen table, reading the newspaper. "Pretty solid win against a good team."

"It's because of Coach Lever," I said. "Guys say he stays late every night watching game films. Every week, he tweaks plays we've already learned. Little things, but they make a big difference."

My dad tapped the newspaper. "The writer thinks Hunter Gates is the difference."

"That's what Hunter thinks too, but it's not just him."

There was a pause. "How about you? Make any plays?"

I shook my head. "Not really. I got two balls thrown to me. The first one blew around in the wind and I couldn't adjust. The second one got knocked down."

My dad opened his hands. "That just means you'll get four next week," he said.

But I didn't. Not in game three, not in game four, not in game five, not in game six. We won them all, moving up to number sixteen in the state rankings. That was a big deal; if we could finish the season at sixteen, we'd qualify for the playoffs.

Mostly I stood on the sidelines while other guys scraped and clawed out the victories. When I did play, it was always to run deep routes that pulled a cornerback and a safety with me. I was never wide open, not with two guys covering me, so Hunter threw underneath to Colton or Ty every time, or else he hit Skeeter with a swing pass. "You'll get your chance," Coach Lever said. "Just be patient."

At school, those were good days. Richie and I were part of an undefeated football team. So what if I was just a decoy? So what if Richie hadn't kicked a game-winning field goal? The Fear the Fag stuff had been pushed under the rug. We were headed to the state playoffs, so we walked the halls with a little swagger.

On the Monday after our sixth victory, the intercom beeped during English class, and Richie was called to the office. His face went pale and my chest felt hollow—had something happened to his mother?

It turned out that the *Seattle Times* wanted to feature him in an article. "The reporter saw that I'd kicked some field goals," Richie said at chess club, "and she remembered my name from the architecture contest and from some violin competitions."

"And that's why she wants to interview you?" I said.

Anya looked at me in amazement. "*Hello, Brock.* How many football players are concert violinists, win architectural design contests, and play top-notch chess?"

CHAPTER 15

My dad was making his way to his van as I came downstairs Wednesday morning. "There's an article about Richie in the sports section," he said as he left. "It's on the table. That kid is truly amazing."

CROWN HILL'S WONDER BOY the headline read. Below was a picture of Richie standing behind his model, a football in one hand and his violin in the other. The article described his achievements in violin, design, math, chess, soccer, football, and even Chinese.

I was happy for him at first, but as I read the article a second time I started to feel sick. It was too much, and it was too much right in your face. The reporter made it seem as if Richie was the only student at Crown Hill who accomplished anything.

At school, the resentment was there, just as I feared it would be. Kids in the hallways called him "Wonder Boy," shouting out, "Cure cancer yet?" "Going to Mars this weekend?" "Seahawks make an offer?" Everything was said with a smile, but all of it had a needle.

Richie knew it, too. At the end of the school day, as we were walking to practice, I could feel how tense he was. That's when Hunter came over. "How did you get that article?"

"What?" Richie said.

"Did you call the *Seattle Times*? Tell them how great you are?"

I moved between them. "He didn't call anybody."

Hunter turned his eyes to me. "That article should be about me. What's he got—three field goals and some extra points? That's nothing. We're undefeated because of me."

Richie pushed me aside. "Maybe people aren't interested in a one-trick pony like you. Maybe they want to read about somebody with real talent."

Hunter stared, amazed. "What did you call me?"

"A one-trick pony. Do you know what it means, or would you like me to explain it?"

Hunter drew himself up. "Don't push me, Fang."

Richie pointed his finger at Hunter. "You've got that backwards. Don't you push me, because I'm done with being pushed."

Hunter's mouth fell open in amazement. "Are you threatening me?" He turned to me again. "This is unreal. Has he lost his mind?"

"Let's go, Richie," I said, pulling him away. When we reached the parking lot, I took Richie by both shoulders and shook him. "What are you thinking? He's bigger, stronger, and meaner, and he's got a slew of friends just like him. You can't take him on. Just keep your mouth shut and stay clear."

CHAPTER 18

Game seven was going to be a nonleague contest against Bellevue at their field. They were Goliath, the school that had won eleven state titles in the last fifteen years.

Monday's practice had a weird feel to it. Skeeter kept fumbling; Hunter was wild; Colton and Ty didn't catch the passes that were on target. As for me and Hunter—the long passes were never where I thought they would be. It was proof that what Richie had said was true: if you're tight, you can't play.

Coach Lever tried to get us to relax, but nothing worked. An hour into practice, he blew his whistle, called us back into the locker room, and had us sit down.

He paced for a while and then stopped and looked us over. The room was dead quiet. "Okay—Bellevue has won a couple dozen state titles. Good for them. But you're not playing a couple dozen teams. You're playing one team. Their guys put their pants on just like you do."

He paused, scratched his neck, and then smiled. "You know what? I bet some of those Bellevue boys have tiny peckers." We all looked up, not sure we'd heard him right. He held his thumb and his forefinger about half an inch apart. "Peckers this big." Everybody laughed. "You're not afraid of guys with tiny peckers, are you?"

"No," a couple of guys called out.

"Come on, I want to hear it."

"No!" we all screamed.

He held up his hands to silence us. "All right. So stop playing scared."

It worked—a little. When we returned to the practice field that day and the next couple of days, we weren't quite so tight, but we were still a long way from loose.

Then came the injury. It happened after practice on Wednesday. Recruiters had been watching Hunter all through those weeks. They came from schools like Central Washington or Portland State. A coach from Nevada was there that day. He stood off by himself, clipboard in hand.

When practice ended, I stayed after and ran long pass routes while Colton ran short ones. Everything was going fine. Hunter was sharp; his passes were right on target. Then, just when we were about to quit, Colton stepped into a hole. His ankle rolled under his foot, and he collapsed in pain. Mr. Rosen raced out, and so did Coach Lever. I stood next to Hunter and watched as they helped Colton hobble off the field.

Before practice the next day, Coach Lever came over to me. "You told me you wanted passes over the middle?"

I nodded.

"Well, your wish just came true. There's no way Colton's going to be ready. And there's no way we're going to be able to throw long against Bellevue, not with their pass rush. So you're going to start, and you're going to be running quick slants and curls. Everything fast. Okay?"

I nodded, but inside I was panicking.

Bellevue's defense was ferocious. I'd seen the film. Nobody hit like they did. I'd gone the whole season running long clearing patterns. The only time I'd hit the ground was when I'd tripped. And now Lever was sending me into the teeth of the hardest-hitting defense in the state, maybe in the country.

I ran nothing but slants and curls that practice, with Coach Lever watching me. "You can do it," he kept saying, clapping. "Just watch the ball into your hands." I was so nervous that I dropped a bunch of easy balls. Each time, Hunter turned away, disgusted.

When practice ended, I heard Coach Lever call my name. "Come with me," he said. "I want to show you something."

He took me to his office, where he had me sit in a chair as he booted up his computer. "I put this together last night after Colton went down. This is footage of Jerry Rice, the greatest receiver of all time."

I watched as Rice caught a pass from Joe Montana, took one step, and then fell down. Then I watched him make another catch and do the same exact thing. Then another and another and another. One step and then down. Sometimes he didn't even take a step.

Coach Lever stopped the film. "You don't like contact, Brock. Some guys do and some don't." I started to argue, but he put his hand up to silence me. "Hey, it's no big deal. It's smart — why put your body on the line unless you have to? Whenever Jerry Rice sensed he was about to get crushed, he got down and he protected the ball. Rice played a long time, and his brains aren't scrambled. Third and inches, fourth and inches — okay, then I expect you to fight. Otherwise, make the catch and get down. You don't have to be the bravest guy in the world. You just have to be brave enough."

CHAPTER 17

On Friday — game day — the atmosphere at school was electric. As I walked the hallways, kids called out, "Good Luck" and "Beat Bellevue." Posters were taped up on the windows and walls. Everybody believed we could pull off the upset — and why not? We hadn't lost all year, and we had Hunter Gates.

When I was in the hallways, feeling the excitement, I thought we could win too. But when I was alone, dread would hit me. At the big moment of the game, would I pull in my arms or fumble? Would the ball bounce off me for an easy interception? I visualized a thousand ways I could blow the game.

Seattle teams play their games at the Memorial Stadium at Seattle Center, which is sixty-five years old. Everything at Bellevue High School — the cars in the parking lot, the locker rooms, the bleachers, the turf — was shiny new. I wished the game were being played at dingy Memorial Stadium.

The Bellevue band played "The Star-Spangled Banner," a horn sounded, and Richie headed out to the field to kick off. That's when Hunter came over and motioned with his head toward the stands. "At least twenty college coaches are up there. Eastern and U Dub and Wazzu for sure. You can't be a wuss, Brock. Not tonight. You've got to step up."

I wanted to stand up to him, to say something like *You take care of your game and I'll take care of mine.* Instead, I nodded, my heart pounding like he was an elementary school principal who'd caught me running in the hall. "I will, Hunter. I promise."

We won the coin toss. Coach Lever opened the offense by sending Skeeter Washington up the middle twice. The guy was tough, fighting for three yards both times, setting up third-and-four. Hunter called the play—play-action pass. It was Colton's favorite route, but now I was running it.

Hunter's eyes were on me as we broke the huddle. On the sidelines, I could feel Coach Lever watching me too. This was my first test. Fail it, and I might get yanked from the game.

The snap was on two. I took two steps forward and made my cut. The pass was low, at my knees, but I caught it and squeezed it tight as I went to the ground. I heard the whistle just as I took a grazing hit across the back. I looked down the line—just enough for a first down. On the sidelines, Coach Lever pumped his fist my way. Hunter clapped his hands together.

We kept driving, putting together two more first downs. I made another catch, this time on second-on-seven, again on a slant. Hunter was a little off—the pass was slightly behind me—but my catch was good for five yards.

It looked like we'd go right in for a score, or at least a field goal try. On a first-and-ten inside the Bellevue thirty, Coach Lever called for a screen pass. It would have worked, too, but Hunter's pass had way too much steam. It caromed off Skeeter's shoulder pads, high into the air, and came down into the waiting arms of one of the Bellevue linemen, who rumbled about twenty yards before he was hauled down at midfield. The Bellevue band played the fight song as the Bellevue fans went crazy.

The sudden reversal shell-shocked our defense. They were late getting on the field, and they weren't set when Bellevue snapped the ball. The QB faked a handoff to the fullback, dropped back three steps, and fired a pass down the sideline to a wide-open receiver.

Eight seconds.

Touchdown.

The Bellevue fight song again; more wild cheering.

Coach Lever paced the sidelines. "It's just one touchdown. Stay calm. Plenty of time."

Then came more trouble. On the kickoff, one of our linemen was flagged for a block in the back, pushing us back to the ten-yard line. The call was for me to run a quick out. I was open, but Hunter's pass was terrible. Short, wobbly, with no zip. Maybe somebody hit his arm; I didn't see. The cornerback covering me jumped the route, made the interception, and was dancing in the end zone seconds later. Again that Bellevue fight song; again more high-fives in the stands.

Bellevue 14, Crown Hill 0.

It got worse. Hunter fumbled a snap the next time we had the ball. Four plays later—touchdown Bellevue. Then another Hunter interception, this time when he tried to pass as he was being sacked.

We didn't put together a decent drive until five minutes before the half. This time, it was all running plays. Skeeter left, Skeeter up the middle, Skeeter right. Quick hitters, pitchouts, draws. All Skeeter.

Bellevue was in a prevent defense, pretty much giving up four or five yards, letting us march down the field, figuring we'd screw up somehow and turn the ball over, or we'd run out of time and have to try a field goal.

We pushed the ball to the twelve-yard line; we had a

third and inches with less than a minute left. Coach Lever called a time-out. "We're going to run a bootleg," he said to us as we huddled around him. "Brock, you're coming across the field. If you're open, Hunter will hit you with a TD pass. If you're not open, Hunter will run for the first down. Everybody got it?"

I trotted back onto the field. On two, I broke straight upfield and cut across. I was open, wide open, but Hunter couldn't pull the trigger. The sideline was coming up when he finally released the ball. I knew that if I kept going, I'd catch it out of bounds, so I made myself hold up. I reached over the sideline for the ball, caught it, tapped my foot, and then felt a bulldozer smack into my back. I went down hard, flipped over twice, but maintained possession of the ball. I looked to the ref. He stared at me for a long moment, and then his arms went straight up: Touchdown!

Because of my touchdown, we were almost upbeat at halftime, even though we trailed 28–7. "Bellevue isn't beating you," Coach Lever hollered. "You're beating yourselves. Stay in the moment and we can win this game. Believe!" Heading out for the second half, I could sense the adrenaline surging through every player on the team.

But Hunter's nightmare continued. His first handoff to Skeeter was chest high. Skeeter had no chance, and the ball bounced free. Bellevue recovered the fumble and scored two plays later. 35–7. Hunter threw another interception later in the third quarter, and he fumbled in the fourth. The final was 48–7, and a stadium that had been packed was nearly empty when the clock finally showed all zeroes.

On the bus ride back, I sat up front next to Richie. Behind us, we'd hear guys mumbling to one another, everything so soft that no words were distinct.

I didn't like losing the game, but the game hadn't been a loss for me. I'd made six catches; I'd been hit a dozen times. My uniform was ripped; my elbow was bleeding; I had another cut over the bridge of my nose. My body ached, but I felt great.

Back at school, the team filed off the bus like prisoners returning to jail. I could have texted my mom, and she'd have picked us up, but I felt like walking.

As Richie and I headed into the night, we saw Mr. Gates chewing out Hunter as they walked to his SUV. We couldn't hear what he was saying, but we could guess.

Richie nodded toward Mr. Gates. "Hunter falling flat on his face is perfect, if you think about it. Everybody is always kissing his butt. *He's going to be a bigtime college quarterback and then play in the NFL. Blah, blah, blah.* You, too, Brock. You're that way. Well, he sure sucked tonight, didn't he? Big stage, good team, and he sucked spectacularly."

Most of me felt exactly the way Richie did. But part of me felt sorry for Hunter. He'd work for years to become a top quarterback. And then—in the most important game of his life—he'd failed. Richie didn't know the sting of failure, but I did.

CHAPTER 10

If winning cures everything, then losing poisons everything. On Monday, the whole school was down. Had we lost in a close game, we might have stayed in the top sixteen in the state and kept our spot in the playoffs. But getting blown out dropped us all the way to number twenty-five. We'd have to beat both Blanchet and O'Dea to have a chance for the playoffs.

At chess club, Richie was quiet. No jokes, no smiles even. He checkmated the guy he was playing and then sat next to Anya to watch our game. "Is something wrong?" Anya said.

Richie dropped his eyes. "It's my mom. It's going to end soon. My dad told me."

I knew I should say something, but I didn't know what. I felt useless. I made a chess move, though I don't know what it was. Anya pushed a pawn forward. Richie shifted in his chair. "I knew it before he told me. She sleeps all the time, and when she's awake there's something different about her. It's almost like she's not part of the world anymore."

Anya reached over and put her hand on top of Richie's. "I'm sorry," she said.

That was what I'd wanted to say. Just that.

The warning bell rang. Richie tapped the chessboard, looked at Anya, and shook his head. "You could have taken Brock's queen with your knight. It's been there for two moves."

At practice on Monday, we did our normal warm-ups, but there was no life in anyone. Before sending us off to our individual groups, Coach Lever sat us down at midfield. For once, he didn't use the bullhorn. His face was long; his voice dead. "We've got to face the truth, gentleman. No matter how hard it is to admit, we've got to face it."

I'd never seen him look so defeated.

He paced back and forth a few times, breathing in and breathing out loudly. Finally he stopped, leaned forward toward us, and whispered as if he were sharing an incredibly important secret, his eyes looking right and left. "Those Bellevue guys—their peckers are way bigger than I thought." There was a moment of dead silence. Then everyone laughed, a nervous *is-it-okay* laugh. "Not this big," Lever went on, holding his thumb and forefinger half an inch apart. "More like this!" And he threw both arms wide. We howled.

When we finally settled down, he was back to his normal self.

"Games like that happen. They just do. You've got to wipe it from your mind. If we win the next two games, we have the best record in Seattle, and we're in the playoffs. So let's have a great week of practice."

And then it was Friday night. A rainy, windy, bone-chilling Seattle Friday night. I was sitting next to Richie in the dingy locker room at Memorial Stadium that somehow, in spite of the cold, felt just right. A parent volunteer passed out black balaclavas and all-weather gloves. They had small openings for your eyes, nose, and mouth, but otherwise they covered your entire head, giving a tough-guy gangster look to the team. Once guys pulled the balaclavas on, I couldn't recognize anyone, not even Richie. We looked as if we were going to hijack a Brinks truck, not play a football game.

Coach Lever stood in the center of the locker room saying the things he always said. Guys around were listening or not listening, adjusting the balaclava or taking it off. Richie was humming some song, his foot tapping the ground nervously. "Beat Blanchet!" Coach Lever finally shouted. We hollered the words back at him, and then we ran down the aisle that led to the field.

CHAPTER 19

In the locker room, the balaclavas and had seemed stifling. As soon as we stepped onto the field, I wished mine were warmer. A freezing wind was blowing hard throughout warm-ups. I could see Hunter tense when he saw the flags flapping wildly beyond the end zone. What stats could he put in a gale?

In the opening quarter, a first down was a big deal. I caught a couple of three-yard passes. Skeeter had to be careful with the wet ball and the slippery footing, so he wasn't getting much push. We weren't going to drive the length of the field and score, not against the wind and the rain and the Blanchet defense. "Don't fumble!" Coach Lever kept reminding us after each change of possessions. "We can't give away points."

On fourth down on their own forty, Blanchet's kicker dropped into punt formation. It looked like a regular kick, which was why nobody was ready. The kicker faked a punt and then streaked to the right. Our guys rushed up to tackle him. A wide receiver slipped behind our defense; the punter stopped and flung the ball as far as he could. It was an ugly pass, wobbly and blowing in the wind, but the Blanchet guy hauled it in and ran for a touchdown. They missed the extra point, but at the end of the first quarter Blanchet led 6–0.

The score held until just before the half, when Blanchet finally made a mistake. It came after they'd stopped Skeeter inches short of a first down, forcing Richie to punt. The wind was swirling as he launched the football a mile high into the stratosphere. Blanchet's returner should have cleared out of the way, but instead he tried to catch it. The ball bounced off his shoulder pads, and one of our guys fell on it, deep in Blanchet territory.

We were back on the field, juiced by the possibility for a quick score that would give us the lead. A handoff to Skeeter picked up seven. Hunter got another seven yards on a read-option run. A quick hitch pass to Ty netted two. On second and eight, Hunter hit me with a perfect pass on a curl route. I caught the ball and went down, protecting against a fumble, two yards short of a first down. We rushed to the line and ran Skeeter on a quick hitter, trying to get the play off before Blanchet's defense was set. The play would have worked, but Skeeter slipped in the backfield.

Fourth-and-four from the seventeen.

Coach Lever called time out, but he didn't talk to us. He had his arm around Richie, and Richie was nodding his head up and down.

The field goal try was from thirty-five yards out. That doesn't sound far, but in the wind and rain on a sloppy field, it was a long way. Everything had to be perfect. Perfect snap, perfect hold, perfect kick. And it was: Richie kicked a low line drive that bore through the wind like a bullet.

Blanchet 6, Crown Hill 3.

Halftime was all about getting warm. The parent volunteers had space heaters going for hands and feet, and dry pants and jerseys for guys who had the energy to change. Coach Lever said a few words about ignoring the weather, and we were back on the field.

Before the kick, Hunter was pacing around by himself. He had about fifty yards passing and maybe thirty more on the ground—nowhere near what he needed to make an impression on a college coach. The rain and wind had let up a little, but the weather was still miserable.

Neither team could get going in the tough conditions. Richie was outkicking their guy, so we had better field position all through the third quarter and the first half of the fourth, but we couldn't take advantage of it. The score was still 6–3, and as the clock ran down in the fourth quarter, so did our hopes for a playoff spot.

Blanchet was backed up on their own ten-yard line,

facing third-and-four. From the shotgun, their QB clapped his hands, but the snap came low. The football slipped through his hands and started bounding toward the goal line. He turned and chased after it, but instead of falling on the ball, he booted it through the back of the end zone and into the bushes. The refs looked at each other, then made the over-the-head signal that meant *safety*. The scoreboard went to 6–5 — a weird score for a weird football game.

Blanchet had a free kick from the twenty after the safety, and we took over at midfield. I looked at the clock: four minutes remained. This was our last chance. And right then, when we needed to put together a drive, the rain picked up, coming down in sheets, while the wind howled through the nearly empty stadium.

As I huddled up with the other guys, water ran down my helmet and onto my neck and back. My shoes squished with every step. My teeth were chattering and my body was shivering. "Eighty-eight slant on one" was the call. A pass to me.

I took my position on the line and made my break. The ball was perfectly thrown, chest high. I was wearing gloves, but the ball still stung as it hit my frozen hands. I got down before a linebacker had a chance to drill me. First down on the Blanchet thirty-nine. Clock ticking.

We ran Skeeter up the middle, and then Hunter hit him with a little swing pass, setting up third and three.

This time, I ran a curl and dropped to my knees, and there was the ball, perfectly thrown again. Hunter gave me a fist pump. First down at the Blanchet twenty-seven. Two minutes and change left.

I ran the curl again, but this time Hunter's pass was batted down at the line of scrimmage. On second and ten, with the rain pouring down, Skeeter carried four guys to the twenty. One minute thirty seconds left on the clock, two time-outs remaining, third-and-three.

My heart was racing, and I wasn't cold—not anymore. I wanted the ball coming my way, but the play call was an option bootleg for Hunter. He took the snap under center and ran to his right, looking downfield. I ran a crossing pattern, making myself available. I was open, but he didn't throw the ball. Instead, he stopped on a dime and cut back. The Blanchet guys had overpursued. Hunter was in the clear. I watched him race toward the end zone. *Fifteen . . . ten . . . five . . . touchdown!* The twenty people in the stands cheered wildly. Hunter had done it. He'd won the game.

But then I spotted the yellow flag, and I knew why Skeeter was staring at his feet. The referee clicked on his microphone. "Holding. Crown Hill. Ten-yard penalty. Repeat third down."

Third-and-thirteen with fifty-two seconds left to play.

Coach Lever called time out; we huddled around him.

"We don't need a first down, because Richie's going to win this game with a field goal. But that wind is right in his face, so we do need to get him closer. I want a check-down pass to Brock—and, Brock, I want you to fight for every extra inch you can get." He put his finger on my chest. "This is the time."

The whistle blew, ending the time-out. Hunter led us to the line, crouched under center: "Rocket!"

I came across the line and found a seam between the linebackers. Hunter's throw was on target. I made myself watch it into my hands and then wrapped both arms around the ball and turned upfield. After one step, I got hit by a linebacker, but I stayed upright and took a second step and then a third. Finally, when I felt I was going down, I drove hard with my legs to make sure I fell forward.

I got up and looked at the yardage stripes—I'd carried the ball all the way to the twelve-yard line. Richie and the rest of the field goal team were coming on the field. "You can do it," I yelled to him as we passed. He didn't look up; his eyes were focused on the goalposts.

The ref blew his whistle, signaling the ball was in play. The wind was right in Richie's face, and so was the rain. The snap was a little high, but the holder got it down. Richie moved into the ball just like it was practice. Not faster, not slower—just the way I'd seen him do it over and over.

The ball rose up into the sky. You could see it in the lights, raindrops all around it, spinning end over end. It went forward for a while, and then it seemed to balloon straight up in the wind.

Finally, it started down, down, down. The kick was straight, but was it long enough? We waited and waited. Finally, it hit the ground. Both officials threw their hands up in the air. *Good!* It had cleared the post by about a yard. The scoreboard changed to 8–6.

We'd beaten Blanchet!

CHAPTER 20

In the locker room, we cheered and pounded on the lockers before exhaustion hit. The bus ride back to school was almost silent. My mom had told me she'd pick us up if it was raining, and I was glad to see her car in the parking lot. Richie and I piled in and my mom turned the heat up full blast. By the time she reached Richie's house, I'd nearly fallen asleep.

I did sleep late on Saturday. When I went downstairs, my dad was waiting for me. I'd been too tired to tell him about the game the night before. Now I did my best, but when it came to it, there wasn't much to tell. He got it, though. "That's kind of how life is sometimes," he said, smiling. "Just a hard slog. The winner is the one who keeps slogging."

I ate a little—I was too sore to eat much—and then

went to Richie's. He wasn't in the shed, so I circled back and knocked on the front door. His father opened it and led me into the kitchen. Richie was sitting at the table with a math book open, his mother across from him. She was wearing a robe that she pulled tight across her chest when she saw me. Richie's violin case was open, the violin not quite resting properly inside it. Had he been practicing earlier?

"You go," his mother said. "You go be with your friend."

Richie looked to his father, who nodded. He stood, put the violin away properly, and packed his books, and then we headed outside. "What do you want to do?" he asked.

"How about Top Pot Doughnuts? I've got some money."

Ten minutes later, we were drinking mochas, eating maple bars, and watching the cars go in and out of the Office Max parking lot. "That was a great kick, you know. Game on the line. Wind. Rain. That was really something."

"I thought I had plenty of distance, and then the wind came up and I thought it was ten yards short."

"You're going to be the star at school. Game-winning field goal in miserable weather. Pretty impressive."

He tilted his head and smiled. "I'm okay with being the star."

I took a bite of my maple bar and washed it down with some mocha. "You've got to admit—it's worked out. You kicking for the team, I mean."

"Oh, sure, it's worked. But it's all a fraud, too."

"What do you mean?"

"They're laying off me because I can kick. But I'm still the loud-mouthed, brainy Chinese kid with the dumb name, the funny hair, and the black glasses. What I'm really good at—music and math and design—none of it counts."

"Most kids don't think that," I said. "It's just a few. The stuff you're good at counts to me, and it counts to other kids too. They just don't say it out loud because—" I stopped, not sure how to explain.

Richie laughed mockingly. "Because they don't want anyone to think they're like me."

In the hallway Monday morning, some kid saw Richie and screamed, "Fong's the Mon," with a Jamaican lilt. Other kids took up the chant, and Richie went into a Bob Marley stoner shuffle that made everyone laugh.

In my classes, lots of kids lied, claiming they were at the game and had seen Richie's kick. At chess club, Anya asked Richie to describe the kick for her. "Sure," he said. "It was like this—" And then he went on to describe kicking into hurricane winds while monsoon rains gushed from the sky.

When he finished, Anya turned to me. "How bad was it?"

"The wind was probably fifteen miles an hour, and it was a little rainy," I said, my voice flat.

"Fifteen!" Richie shrieked. "It was one hundred and fifteen. Bring me a Bible. Bring me the Qur'an. I'll swear to it. I am Legend."

CHAPTER 21

There was a different vibe at practice during the O'Dea week. All games are tough, but Coach Lever knew that the wind and rain had beaten us up as much as Blanchet had, so he went easy. He locked the weight room. "Your muscles need rest, not stress," he said. We stretched; we jogged; we stretched again. We practiced our plays, but we went at three-quarters speed.

All that week, I saw Hunter's eyes scanning the edge of the practice field, looking for college recruiters. None showed, not even coaches from small schools. Not a single one. It was nearly the end of recruiting season, and he didn't have an offer.

I'd looked at Hunter's statistics in the *Seattle Times*. They weren't bad—he was in the top third in almost everything, but nothing jumped out. Strictly from the numbers, he looked like a pretty good quarterback in a so-so league. He needed to make the playoffs—and play well in the playoffs—to catch a recruiter's eye. The O'Dea game was huge for him.

On Tuesday, in the main entrance, there was a big picture of an X'ed-out Pope Francis with the words BEAT THE CATHOLICS! written in red across his face. Everybody who saw it laughed, but it came down before lunch.

On Wednesday, a warm front came in from Hawaii. On Friday—game day—the temperature was going to be around sixty, and there was no chance of rain. Perfect football weather.

I thought at Thursday's practice we'd watch film and walk through plays, but instead we played five-on-five touch football. "Football is fun," Lever said as he passed out a bunch of Nerf footballs. "Don't forget that."

Colton Sparks was finally back from his injury. "Touch is perfect for you, Brock," he mocked when we were making up teams. "Just the right amount of contact. Besides, you like boys touching you, don't you?"

Some of the guys around me laughed, but there was tension, too. Was I going to let him get away with that? My hands balled into fists. I had to take him on.

And then, suddenly, I didn't have to.

"He did fine while you were injured," Skeeter said in his slow, quiet way.

"He flopped to the ground every time he caught a pass," Colton snapped. "He's a wuss."

"That's not how I remember it," Skeeter said. "I remember him fighting for extra yards in the cold against Blanchet while *you* were on the sidelines in a nice warm parka with your little sore foot wrapped up in a heating pad. So stick a sock in it, Sparks."

Everyone went dead quiet. Nobody had ever seen Skeeter angry before. Finally, Colton motioned toward the other side of the field. "I think I'll play over there," he said. "If you think so much of Ripley, then you can have him on your team."

"I will," Skeeter said, the words somehow menacingly soft.

Colton turned and walked over to another group. Skeeter looked at me for a second. I gave him a nod, and he gave the same back. He didn't have to stick up for me, but he did. And I'll never forget it.

For the next hour, we threw Nerf balls around, playing on short fields in small groups and scoring a million touchdowns. Then Coach Lever sounded the bullhorn and we circled around. "We're going to the game tomorrow as a team, and we're coming back as a team. No driving yourself or going with your parents. Win or lose, we stay together. We're family."

I liked Coach Lever more than any coach I'd had in

any sport. He wanted the "family" stuff to be true, but it just wasn't. When the season ended, what would happen to Richie? Would Hunter and those guys leave him alone? That was the best Richie could hope for, and that's not "family."

CHAPTER 22

"You know how much I'd like to go to the game, but—"

That's what my dad said to me Thursday night at dinner.

I pushed my mashed potatoes around. "It's okay. You don't have to explain."

"I'll be listening on the radio. I'll be seeing you that way."

The radio was news to me. "Our game is on the radio?"

"Yeah. KHSS does the top prep game every Friday night, and this week it's yours. The winner will make the state tournament; the loser is out. What game could be bigger than that?"

"I'd listen," my mom said, "but my nerves can't take it."

"There's nothing to worry about," I said. "Colton Sparks is back. They'll send him over the middle. I'll run long and hope Hunter throws to me a couple of times."

"Well, I hope he doesn't. I want you to win because I know how hard you've worked, but it would be okay with me if you lost and didn't make the playoffs."

School dragged on Friday. When it ended, I went home, ate a small meal, and played video games until it was time to head back to catch the school bus to Seattle Center.

I'd arranged with Richie to walk with him. He came out before I knocked, but I could see past him into the living room. A woman who looked like a nurse was sitting across from Richie's father. She had some papers out, and she was pointing to something on the page.

As we headed toward school, it seemed wrong to ask Richie about his mom, but it seemed wrong to talk about anything else, so I stayed silent. We'd gone a block when he spoke. "I just wish it would end."

I swallowed. "Should you stay home? I mean . . ." My voice trailed off.

"To be with her when she dies?" Richie shook his head. "It's not her anymore. She's on morphine. My dad gives her way more than he's supposed to, but the nurse says it's fine, so I guess it is. She's asleep most of the time, but when she is awake and talking, it's all crazy stuff. Last week, she told me not to let them chop my head off. I hate being with her when she's like that, and my dad doesn't want me to hear it either." He stopped, then laughed a little. "The last time I really talked to her was Wednesday morning. She told me to win the kickball game on Friday. I've told her a thousand times it's called football, but she can never remember." He paused. "I like that conversation. I can live with that one being the last one."

"You'll still go to Pittsburgh, won't you? I mean, even if . . ."

"Yeah, I'll still go. My dad wants me to win—that's just how he is. But he's hyperfocused on getting back to Nanjing. I'll be living in China by the New Year."

We'd reached the school parking lot. About fifty yards away, guys were clumped together in small groups. Coach Lever's bullhorn blared, and his voice followed. "All right, gentleman. Time to get on the bus."

CHAPTER 2[illegible]

Friday traffic made the ride to the Seattle Center Coliseum slow. Coach Lever kept looking at his watch and then at the road, but we'd left early, so we arrived in plenty of time. Once we were suited and ready to go, Coach Lever called us to attention. He gave his normal pep talk about never quitting and being a band of brothers, but he talked faster and louder than usual.

When he finished, Skeeter—who was usually super-quiet—had us form a circle. He screamed: *"Who let the dogs out?"* And we all shouted back: *"Woof, woof, woof, woof, woof!"*

We did it three times, and then Skeeter let out a howl and we ran through the dirty old runway that led onto the field. After that, it was stretches . . . warm-ups . . . the national anthem . . . game time.

O'Dea's head coach knew Coach Lever liked to get Skeeter going with the run in the first quarter, so on our first few drives O'Dea brought seven guys up close. With the box full of defenders, Skeeter was stuffed at the line. Colton ran a few quick curls to try to soften the defense, but he dropped one and fell to his knees controlling the other. Our first two possessions were three-and-outs.

O'Dea put together two decent drives, but twice on fourth down our defense held. When we got the ball for a third time, the score was still 0–0.

The first-down call was for a run, but O'Dea again brought their linebackers up close. At the line of scrimmage, Hunter changed the play, dumping the run in favor of a play-action pass.

The ball was supposed to go to Colton on a crossing pattern, but Colton slipped on his first step and went down. I looked back, knowing I was Hunter's second option. Their cornerback had me in single coverage, but the guy was fast, so I hadn't created much separation. Hunter threw to me anyway, counting on me to win the fight for the ball.

The throw hung in the air, so the O'Dea guy had a shot at an interception. The pass hit him in the hands, but he couldn't hang on. The ball tumbled end over end in the air. I watched it and watched it, and then it was in my hands, the O'Dea cornerback was sprawled on the ground, and I was off to the races.

Touchdown!

* * *

One of the strangest things about football is that a game can be a defensive struggle for a quarter or even a half, and then one team scores, and after that first touchdown the offenses come to life.

After my TD, O'Dea came at our defense with everything in their playbook. They ran a reverse for twenty-five yards on first down, followed that with a couple of counter plays for another first down, and then finished the drive with a thirty-yard halfback pass for the game-tying TD.

Hunter returned full of confidence. He hit two passes to Colton over the middle and a bubble screen to Ty Erdman, and then—when O'Dea was thinking pass—Skeeter ripped off thirty yards on a draw. Two plays later, Colton caught a fade in the corner of the end zone, putting us back on top.

Our lead didn't last. Back and forth both teams went, rolling over the defenses. Hunter was having his best game at the absolute most important moment—putting up eye-popping numbers. His passes were like guided missiles. I had three catches, and Ty and Colton had more. And at the very moment Hunter was playing lights out, our defense was having its worst game.

The score was 21–21 at the half.

Coach Lever jumped up on a bench in the locker room during halftime. "Isn't this great?" he shouted, clapping his hands. "Soak it in. Make the plays, be a winner." Then he paused. "Only how about we play some damn defense!"

The defensive guys huddled. They pounded on one another's shoulder pads, screamed about how they were not only going to stop O'Dea but stomp on them. And then O'Dea took the second-half kickoff, drove the length of the field in a half-dozen plays, and scored.

Hunter didn't flinch. Skeeter was forgotten as Coach Lever called pass play after pass play. Ty and Colton handled the short and medium stuff; I hauled in a couple more long bombs. There was no stopping us . . . but there was no stopping them, either.

28–28.

35–28.

35–35.

Midway through the fourth quarter, O'Dea had the ball on their own thirty-seven. On our sidelines, Coach Lever kicked at the fake grass. Our defense hadn't held them in nearly three quarters; why would we be able to stop them now?

And we didn't, but they stopped themselves. The mistake came on a bubble screen to the left side. The receiver caught the pass but started to run before tucking the ball away. One of our linebackers put his helmet right on the football as he made the tackle. The ball popped loose, and another one of our guys fell on it.

Turnover!

I raced onto the field, expecting we'd march down and take the lead with another touchdown. Hunter was in the zone, and all of us were in the zone with him. I caught a first-down pass for fifteen yards to the twenty. Skeeter ran a sweep for eight, setting up second-and-two. Ty caught a little curl for another first down on the six. We were unstoppable, a big tank rolling across an empty field.

Then came an offside penalty, pushing us back to the eleven. Colton dropped a pass; Skeeter was strung out for no gain. On third-and-goal, Hunter tried to hit me on a fade to the corner, but his pass carried me out-of-bounds.

That made it fourth down—it was up to Richie.

As he ran onto the field, my heart wasn't thumping; it was trying to come completely out of my chest. It was a twenty-eight-yard field goal—no wind and no rain. But could he handle the pressure? Fans were screaming from both sides. I couldn't watch, but I couldn't *not* watch.

The snap was good; the hold was good; the kick was pure. Right down the middle with twenty yards to spare.

Crown Hill 38, O'Dea 35.

On the sidelines, everybody went berserk, pounding Richie so hard, he covered his head. One defensive stop and we'd make the state playoffs.

I give it to the O'Dea guys—there was no panic in that final drive. They came out as if it were the first quarter, mixing up passes and runs, working their way methodically down the field, chewing up the clock. They wanted to score with as little time left as possible, leaving Hunter no time to work magic.

A screen pass, a run, another run—first down on their forty-two. Five minutes left.

A run, a pass—first down on our forty-three. Four minutes left.

A screen pass, a run, a run—first down on our twenty-eight. Two thirty left.

A QB draw, a flanker reverse—first down on our thirteen. One-twenty left.

And then we got lucky.

On a play-action pass, the O'Dea quarterback delivered a strike into the end zone. Their tight end had the ball hit his hands and then pop up in front of his eyes. He reached for it, and then he had it for a second time, and then he bobbled it again, and it slipped away, and we were still in the game.

Two fullback runs followed: smash-mouth football, right up the gut, pushing the ball to our four, setting up fourth down and a yard with twenty seconds on the clock.

"Time out!" Coach Lever called.

He had all of us gather around him, offense and defense. "Okay," he shouted, "get low, drive hard. One play. Win this mother-sucker!"

Those of us who weren't on the field hooked our arms

and screamed across the grass, urging our defense to hold them. There'd be no field goal try.

This was it—do or die.

O'Dea came out in a power formation. Our lineman pawed at the ground, ready to drive forward, like horses in the starting gate. The O'Dea QB took the snap, turned, and handed it to their fullback. He hit the pile . . . pushed . . . pushed . . . and was pushed back.

The ref blew his whistle and waved his arms. The line judge laid the ball down, looked toward the first-down markers, turned, and signaled that it was our ball, first and ten.

We'd stopped them.

We'd won!

Only we hadn't. Not yet. We still had to run out the clock, and they had all their time-outs left.

Coach Lever sent out his short-yardage team, leaving me on the sidelines standing next to Richie.

On first down, Hunter took a knee on the three-yard line.

O'Dea called time. Eleven seconds left.

Another knee; another O'Dea time-out. Seven seconds left.

A third knee; the final O'Dea time out. Three seconds left.

Coach Lever called us all around him, but he was

yelling only at Richie, hollering over the deafening crowd noise, explaining the strategy. "Go into punt formation, but don't punt it. Just let the clock run out, and then kneel down. Understand? Whatever you do, don't punt it. A safety won't hurt us. Understand? Wait until you see zeroes, and then kneel."

Richie nodded and raced onto the field. The O'Dea guys were up on the line, ready to charge like wild bulls.

The snap was a good one. Richie caught it; he moved a step to his left, but there was no strong rush. Our line was holding. The scoreboard clock counted down the numbers.

00:02

00:01

00:00.

I heard the horn, and then I saw Richie throw the ball high in the air and run to join the mob of guys jumping crazily along the sideline.

We'd won!

Our fans roared in delight as O'Dea's crowd sank into silence. Then, as we celebrated, the head referee started blowing on his whistle and wildly waving his arms.

What was going on?

The officials all huddled, and suddenly the O'Dea side was cheering. Their roar started slowly, but then it grew steadily louder and louder. Finally, the O'Dea players started hugging each other. I looked at the scoreboard and it read O'Dea 41, Crown Hill 38.

All of us were looking around, mouths open and eyes wide, totally confused. What had happened?

But I knew.

In my mind, I saw that final play, only this time in slow motion.

The clock had wound down to 00:00, but that didn't mean the game was over. Not in football. The game isn't over in football until the player goes down or out-of-bounds.

Richie did neither. He threw the ball up in the air like you do in a soccer or basketball game, and an O'Dea lineman, standing in the end zone, caught it. The O'Dea guy didn't know it was an interception. He didn't know he'd scored a game-winning touchdown. He just caught the football because it was coming down and he was standing there.

I looked onto the field. Coach Lever, his face bright red, his eyes almost coming out of his head, was facing the referee, begging for an explanation. The ref pointed to the end zone. He pantomimed Richie throwing the ball in the air and the O'Dea player catching it. Lever's shoulders sank; and I knew I was right.

It was over.

Only it wasn't.

CHAPTER 24

"Was it me?" Richie asked as we headed off the field. "Did I do something?"

"It wasn't your fault," I said, my voice low.

"But what did I do? I don't get it."

"It's a weird football rule. I'll explain later."

We trailed off to the locker room, moving like zombies. Once we were there, everyone sat stunned, including Coach Lever. Finally he snapped out of it, at least a little. "We win as a team and we lose as a team," he said, his voice flat. "I don't want anyone blaming anybody. Understand?"

As he talked, eyes peered over at Richie.

We sat together on the bus and I explained the rule, my voice just audible over the hum of the engine. "But you shouldn't blame yourself. Half the guys on the team don't know that rule."

"Yeah? Well, who do you think Hunter is going to blame?"

My head was throbbing. One minute we were headed to the playoffs, and Hunter was going to get his chance to shine under the big lights. The next minute, we weren't in the playoffs, and all the lights were out.

All because of Richie.

That's how he'd see it.

What would he do? And how could I stop him from doing it?

As the bus bumped along Aurora Avenue, I caught glimpses of Lake Union through the gaps between apartment buildings, the darkness of the water outlined by the light from houses and businesses.

I didn't want the bus ride to end. I wanted us to keep going and going, up into Shoreline and then Edmonds and Lynnwood and Bellingham and British Columbia and Alaska. I wanted it to bump along until everyone had forgotten everything. But the driver exited on Sixty-Fifth, by Woodland Park, drove up and over Phinney Ridge, braked at the stop sign by the violin shop, rolled past the Goodwill store, and turned into the Crown Hill High parking lot.

"Stay clear of Hunter," I said as the bus hissed to a stop.

Richie cocked his head sideways. "I told you I'm not afraid of him. Not anymore."

We climbed off the bus and walked in the silent darkness toward his house. It wasn't late—just after ten—but it seemed as if the world had already gone to sleep. We'd made it one block when a dark SUV with tinted windows flew by, its headlights piercing the darkness, the roar of its engine breaking the night silence. The SUV circled the block and drove by again, only this time slowly.

"Do you recognize it?" Richie asked.

"I don't think so. Do you?"

He shook his head. "No."

The SUV didn't circle a third time, but we did hear it speed off into the night, tires squealing. After that, the only sounds were our footfalls on the concrete, step by step.

There was no moon and no stars, and so many trees that—despite the street lamps—the sidewalk was almost black. I kept looking for the headlights of that SUV, dreading the headlights, but the dark street stayed dark.

Finally, we reached Richie's block. His was the sixth house down. Parked a few houses down on the other side of the street was a dark SUV with tinted windows. "Is that it?" Richie asked.

Was it? I didn't know. My heart was pounding. "Maybe."

We both walked at a steady pace as we passed the SUV—careful not to go faster or slower. The SUV seemed empty. We crossed the street and approached Richie's house. It, too, was dark and silent—his mother asleep, his father asleep, the hospice worker gone home.

And then a light went on in his shed. Richie looked at me. "That's not my dad. Not now."

The light went off.

Before I could stop him, he turned and raced toward his shed. I ran behind. In the dim light cast by the street lamps, I could see that the shed door was slightly open. He always kept it closed and locked.

Richie pushed the door fully open and stepped inside; I came seconds behind. He'd flicked the light back on and was staring at the ground.

For a long moment, I didn't understand what I was seeing. What were all those little things on the floor?

Then I knew, and my breathing stopped.

They'd turned it over. They'd turned it over and then they'd smashed it to bits, smashed it and then stepped on it and then smashed it some more.

"Richie," I said, grabbing his arm and trying to pull him out. "Richie— "

That's when the shed door closed.

There were four of them. I couldn't see their faces because they had balaclavas on—the ones from the Blanchet game. All I could see were eyes and noses and mouths. One of them stepped forward, paused for a long moment, and then pushed Richie hard in the chest.

"Stop it," I yelled, and the biggest guy grabbed me,

kicked my legs out from under me, wrestled me to the ground, and shoved my face down onto the concrete floor. Then he stuck his knee in my back to keep it there.

I couldn't move, but I could still see. A second guy pushed Richie hard, hurling him back across the shed. "Leave him alone," I choked out, and then a gloved hand shoved a rag in my mouth, a rag that smelled like glue, and I was gasping for air as they pushed Richie again and again, taking turns. They didn't speak. Not one of them said a word. But they laughed, a growling laugh, a hyena's laugh. Richie tried to fight back, but he could never get his balance. After about a dozen shoves, he fell, and then they circled around him and kicked at his stomach. He pulled his legs to his chest and covered his head, but they still kicked, and they still laughed.

Finally they stopped. They stood over him, all three breathing heavily, tense. The guy pinning me down moved his knee and relaxed his hand. I spit the rag out of my mouth, rolled over, and gulped air. I tried to stand, but now another guy's foot was against my chest, pressing me down to the floor. His eyes darted this way and that. Then, on some invisible signal, they took off—all of them scrambling to get out of the shed, up the driveway, and into the street. The SUV started up, the tires squealed, and they were gone.

Richie rolled over onto his knees, and I helped him to his feet. His face was streaked with dirt.

"Are you okay?" I asked. He nodded and took a step forward, his hand clutching his gut. "Stay here. I'll get your dad and he can take you to a hospital."

"No," Richie said. "Don't get my dad."

"You might have broken ribs."

"I'm okay."

"How do you know? You need x-rays."

"I just know," he said, his voice angry.

He took a step toward the door. I tried to help him, but he pushed me away, so I walked by his side as he made his way to his front porch.

"This isn't right," I said as he slipped the key into the lock. "You need to see a doctor."

"Go home, Brock. Just go home."

CHAPTER 2[illegible]

My father had waited up. He was sitting in his chair, a reading lamp next to him, the rest of the house in darkness. He put down his book as I entered. "Tough loss," he said. "Really tough loss."

"Yeah, it was." He wanted to talk about the game, but for me the game had happened a million years ago. I let a few seconds tick by. "I'm really tired, Dad. Can we talk in the morning?"

He nodded. "Sure. I understand."

"Thanks." I started toward the stairs.

"Wait a second, Brock." I turned back, and I saw his eyes measure me. "Is something wrong? Something else besides the game?" My throat went dry, and I could feel my shoulders slump. "Just tell me," he said, his voice open and honest.

"The guys blame Richie."

His face relaxed. "Well, the guys are wrong. It was your coach's mistake."

I looked at him, confused.

"Think it through," he went on. "Richie wasn't going to punt, right? So why have him on the field? With the game on the line, you don't put the ball in the hands of your least experienced player. Hunter should have been back in punt formation. He knows the rules. Your coach will see his mistake and—if he's the kind of man you say he is—he'll take the blame. It's on him, not Richie."

As my dad spoke, I realized he was one hundred percent right but that it didn't matter. "It's too late," I said.

It was his turn to be confused. "How can it be too late? The game ended two hours ago."

The clock on the mantel ticked. A car drove past the house.

"They beat up Richie after the game. They were in the shed behind his house. We saw a light and went back there, and they were waiting for him."

"Who did it?"

"They had balaclavas on, so I couldn't see their faces. And they didn't say anything, either. But it was Hunter and Colton and a couple of his friends. I'm sure of it."

"How bad?"

"Richie was wearing a heavy coat, and they were wearing gloves and didn't hit him in the face, but they knocked him around pretty good. And they smashed up his model."

He went quiet for a while, and then he spoke. "How about you? Did they do anything to you?"

"No, they just held me down."

"Nobody hit you?"

"No."

My dad folded his hands in front of him. His breathing was deep and slow. Finally, he looked up at me. "So what are you going to do?"

I shrugged. "Richie doesn't want to tell anybody."

"Brock, I didn't ask what *Richie* was going to do. I asked what *you* were going to do."

My chest went tight. I hadn't thought of it in that way. I looked at my dad, and his eyes held mine. He didn't say anything more; he didn't rush me. Thoughts swirled around in my head, and then things came clear. "I'll tell Coach on Monday. I'll tell him everything."

"You don't think you should call your principal or vice principal tonight? Or email them?"

"No, I tried with Mr. Spady before when Hunter and those guys hassled Richie, and he didn't do anything. But Coach won't let it ride."

"What about the police?"

"What can they do? I didn't see anybody's face. I didn't hear anybody's voice. And Richie doesn't want a bunch of police in his house asking questions, not with his mother sick like she is. I know he doesn't."

My dad thought for a while. "Is it safe to wait until Monday to talk to your coach? What if they go after Richie again?"

"They'll hassle him some at school on Monday, but they won't do anything more."

In my room, I lay on my bed and stared at the ceiling, thinking about what had happened. I saw those guys pushing Richie back and forth. I heard their laughter. I saw his model flipped over, the pieces strewn on the floor. I didn't think I'd ever fall asleep, but then the room started whirling around. My thoughts got jumbled and turned into bad dreams, and the next thing I knew it was late morning and a hard rain was pounding against my window.

"Are you okay?" my mom said when I made my way downstairs. She was sitting at the kitchen table. I could tell from the tone of her voice and the look of concern in her eyes that she knew everything.

"I'm fine," I said.

She stood and kissed me on the forehead. "You need to eat something," she said.

"I'll eat later," I replied, heading for the door. I looked around. "Where's Dad?"

"He's at the bank. The manager called and said they needed him. They haven't called him on Saturday for a long time."

CHAPTER 20

Ten minutes later, I was at Richie's house. An unfamiliar car was parked in front—probably the hospice person's. All the curtains were pulled closed, both upstairs and downstairs. Two newspapers sat in their plastic covering on the lawn, untouched. In the misty grayness, the whole house looked sick.

Part of me wanted to turn around and go straight home. I had to wait a long time before Richie's father answered. "He's still in his room. That football game very rough. He's very sore."

"Can I see him?"

"No. He not see anyone. He rest."

I nodded. "Tell him I'll come by tomorrow. Okay?"

His father shook his head. "No, don't come tomorrow. Richie's mother is very, very sick. He spend Sunday with her. You are a good friend to Richie. Thank you."

The door closed.

On the walk home, I took out my phone and texted Richie. *You okay?* I typed. I waited, staring at the screen, but no text came back. I put my phone on vibrate, shoved it back in my pocket, and zipped up my jacket.

I started thinking about Monday. I wanted to believe Coach Lever was different from Mr. Spady. But was he? Would Hunter deny it all, and then would Coach Lever look at me and shrug? Was that how it would end?

I closed my eyes and tried not to think of anything, but it didn't work. The balaclavas . . . the gloves . . . the smashed model . . . Richie huddled on the ground . . . his mother bowing as she handed me strange desserts. A new image would crowd out an old one, stay a second or two, and then be crowded out in turn.

CHAPTER 27

As I walked to Richie's on Monday morning, my stomach was in a knot. He'd have a parade of reasons why I shouldn't say anything to Coach Lever. I tried to plan what I'd say back to him, but who was I kidding? I wasn't going to win an argument with Richie. I'd just have to do what I needed to do no matter what he said.

I turned the corner, looked down the block toward his house, and knew. Cars were parked up and down the street and in his driveway. The front door to his house was open, and a small woman was walking up the porch steps, a bouquet of white flowers in her hand. Another car pulled up, and an Asian man and woman got out.

Richie's mother was dead.

I stopped fifty yards from the house, wondering what to do. With so many people in the house, would his father want me—a white kid—inside? Would Richie want me?

I could come back another time, I thought. But Richie

might never return to Crown Hill, and I needed to tell him how sorry I was. I didn't want to do that with a text or an email.

I moved closer to the house, staying on the opposite side of the street. The curtains were pulled back for the first time in months. Eight or ten adults were standing in a group, talking. Richie's dad was one of them, but I didn't see Richie.

I walked across the street to get a better look, and that's when Richie's father looked out the window and spotted me. A moment later, he rushed out of his front door, motioning me to come closer to him.

"You. Richie's friend."

I nodded. "Yes."

"His mother has died."

I nodded again. "Can I talk to him?"

"No. He's not here. You come with me."

Before I knew what was happening, he grabbed my elbow and pulled me around the side of the house and toward the shed. When we reached it, he threw open the door and motioned for me to look. Richie's model was still in pieces on the floor.

His father turned to me. "Why would Richie do this?"

I was confused. What was he talking about? And then I understood. Richie had told his father that he'd destroyed his own work.

Before I had to answer, his father spoke again. "I asked him if he did it out of sadness or anger. He wouldn't answer. Do you know why he did this? You are his friend. Why would he do this?"

"Where is he?" I asked, ignoring the question.

His father threw his hands up. "He went to school. His mother is dead and he goes to school. I tell him to stay home and to grieve, but he says he must go one more time, and then never again. He has something important to do, he says. I say, more important than to grieve for your mother? He says he owes someone something. He is angry when he speaks. I never see him angry like this. Never."

"How long ago did he leave?" I ask, my heart pounding so fast, I could feel my pulse in my temples.

"Five minutes." His father motioned to the floor again. "Why would Richie do this?"

My eyes rose from the destruction on the floor to the shelf that held the mahogany box.

I looked at his father. His face, his eyes, everything about him, was confused.

Five minutes.

I turned, pushed past Richie's father, dropped my backpack, and started running.

Five minutes.

I ran—remembering how my father used to run—at

a steady pace. My eyes scanned the area in front of me, hoping to see Richie around the next corner, or the next.

When I reached the large parking lot in front of the main entrance to the school, I stopped and looked around, breathing heavily, sweat dripping down the side of my face. Everything seemed normal. But then I heard something that sounded like a car backfiring.

Seconds later, kids came racing out of all the exits, heading in all directions, just running out and away. I took a few cautious steps toward the school, weaving my way through. I grabbed a kid from my English class. "What's going on?" I shouted.

He looked back over his shoulder. "It's that Fang kid. He's got a gun, and he's got Hunter and Colton and some other guys trapped in a bathroom. He's going to kill them."

I was fighting to get into the school, but moving forward was hard because so many kids were rushing right at me. A teacher grabbed me. "Get away from the building," she screamed.

I shook her off and plunged forward. Now fewer kids were in front of me so I could move more easily. As I reached the steps to the main entrance, I heard, in the distance, police sirens. They sounded far off, but they were only minutes away.

I opened the doors to the school and looked left and

right. The main hallways were deserted. Where was he? How would I find him? Then I heard Richie's voice. "Lie down!" he was screaming. "You hear me? Lie down!"

His voice was coming from the hallway leading to the boys' gym. I ran toward his voice. I'd taken about twenty steps when I heard a gunshot that echoed repeatedly down the long hallway. I stopped. "Don't! Don't! Don't!" someone screamed, and then I heard sobbing.

I ran again, but slower, my knees weak.

And then I was there.

Three thin metal garbage cans were lined up side by side like shiny soldiers in front of the entrance to the boys' bathroom. There was no way to slip past them without making noise—they were Richie's warning devices.

The police sirens grew louder, and below their high-pitched wail I could hear Hunter and Colton and the rest of them, sobbing softly and mumbling words I couldn't make out. I reached out to the closest garbage can and rattled it loudly.

Richie's voice filled the silence. "You come in here and I'll shoot them. I'll shoot them all."

"It's me, Richie. It's Brock. I want to help."

Silence.

"I want to help," I repeated.

"I don't want your help. I don't want anybody's help. Go away."

Police cars pulled to screeching stops at the main entrance. I heard doors opening and then slamming shut. The sounds were muffled, distant, but I knew what was coming. At Columbine, the cops had waited outside and kids had died inside. The cops didn't wait anymore. They'd be coming in fast, and they'd be coming after Richie. If the police saw him with a gun in his hands, they'd kill him. They'd fire and he'd be dead. Was that what he wanted?

"I'm coming in, Richie."

He fired another shot. I jumped back as the sound reverberated off the tile and the porcelain and the metal, echoing and echoing until it sounded like twenty shots.

Terrified voices mingled with the echoes. "Don't!" . . . "I'm sorry!" . . . "Stop!"

From down the hallway, I could hear heavy footsteps approaching. Time was running out. I pushed the garbage cans aside and stepped into the bathroom.

Hunter and Colton and two other guys whose faces I couldn't see were lying on their stomachs. Richie was standing over them, holding his gun with two hands but still shaking violently. He looked at me, and then he looked back at them.

"Richie," I said softly, "it's over. Give me the gun."

The footsteps kept coming toward us, closer and closer. It wasn't a matter of minutes; it was a matter of seconds.

I took a step forward.

"Get out of here, Brock!"

"They'll kill you."

"I don't care."

Hunter lifted his face from the floor. "Please, please, please. I'm sorry. Don't." Richie pointed the gun at his head. Hunter covered his head with his hands and sobbed.

The police were just outside the bathroom door. I could hear them breathing.

I took a step toward Richie, reached out, and put my hand on the wrist of his gun hand. Richie turned so that the gun was pointing right at me, his arm rigid. "Let go, Richie," I whispered.

His eyes stared into mine; his grip stayed firm. I heard a policeman slide a garbage can aside. Time had run out. I put my other hand on the gun itself and twisted. He held tight for one long second, and then his hand relaxed.

I had the gun.

"Go!" I screamed to Hunter and Colton and the two other guys. "Get out of here!" And they were up and out, running to the safety of the police.

From the hallway, there was noise and shouting, and then everything went quiet. That's when I realized I was holding the gun. I knelt down, placed the gun gently on the floor, and then slid it to the very back corner of the bathroom. "We're coming out!" I hollered. "Nobody has a gun."

"Walk slowly," a voice answered. "And keep your hands where we can see them."

When it came to it, I almost had to carry Richie out. His feet had nearly stopped working; his head hung on his chest; his body sagged. I felt drained and weak, but together we took those ten steps. We stepped into the hallway—our hands raised—and instantly my face was against a locker, and a second later I was down on the floor and Richie was down on the floor and we were both being handcuffed. My shoulders felt like they were going to come out of their sockets, and I'd hit the floor so hard, I felt dizzy, but I was alive and Richie was alive and Hunter Gates was alive and everyone was alive, so no matter how much it hurt, it didn't hurt at all.

CHAPTER 2[illegible]

It was over, but it wasn't. For the rest of the morning, I answered questions at the police station, with my mom and dad sitting behind me. When the police were done, my parents took me home, and they made me go over everything again. At one point, my dad interrupted to say I'd done a brave thing, and my mom turned on him. "He could have been killed," she said, her eyes filled with angry tears. A few minutes later, my mom told me she was proud of me, and it was my dad who told me I should have waited for help.

At both the police station and home, I tried to find out about Richie. How was he? Where was he? When could I talk to him? Nobody—not the police, not my parents—had answers. When I finally got upstairs to my own room, the first thing I did was open my laptop and email him: *Write me.*

I hit send, and a second later a mailer-daemon message popped up on my screen telling me that my message had been addressed to an invalid email address.

His account had been shut down.

Crown Hill High was closed the next day and would reopen on Wednesday with an all-school assembly. My parents wanted to stay home with me, but when I told them I needed some time to myself, they didn't argue. I ate breakfast and then headed to Richie's house. I was sure he wasn't there, but I hoped to talk to his father. I knocked on the front door, waited, knocked again, and then gave up.

I walked down the porch steps and around back to the shed. I tried the doorknob—expecting it to be locked—but it turned, so I stepped inside.

The plywood base for Richie's model was back up on the table. Richie's father must have done that. He'd also taken some of the pieces that weren't smashed and placed them on the board: a section of the new wing, a few trees, three benches, the back parking lot. Other pieces were lying on their sides. I picked up a couple and tried to remember where they belonged. After a few attempts, I stopped.

Chemotherapy couldn't keep Richie's mom from

dying. A stationary bicycle won't keep my dad's muscles from wasting away. Some things go wrong and stay wrong, and nothing anyone can do will ever make them right. I left the shed, pulling the door closed behind me, and went home.

PART FIVE

EPILOGUE

CHAPTER

My parents told me I didn't have to go back to school until I felt ready, but I had to return sometime—Wednesday was as good as any other day.

The morning assembly lasted half an hour. Mr. Spady spoke first, then Coach Lever. Ms. Levine, the special ed teacher, was last. She challenged us to transform Crown Hill High into a place of love. A few guys in the back snickered, saying they were all for it, but most kids stared ahead, their elbows on their knees, their chins resting in their hands.

As I walked the hall that week, a few kids called out, "Hey, good to see you," and "Brock, my man." Most kids stayed clear of me. I was a hero, the guy who'd taken the gun away from a school shooter. But I was also the shooter's best friend. So who was I, really?

Thursday night, my dad told me Richie was being held at the Juvenile Detention Center near Capitol Hill.

I wanted to go see him, or at least call him and talk to him, but my dad shook his head. I wasn't a member of his family. That meant I couldn't phone him—ever—and I could visit him only on Saturday afternoons, and then only for thirty minutes.

I went online after dinner and found a photo of a room at the JDC. Concrete floor. A thin mattress on top of a long board that was wedged into the wall. A single shelf above the mattress. A tiny window above the shelf. It seemed impossible that Richie was there, but he was.

On Saturday afternoon, as my mom wound her way across town, I thought of how much I wanted to see Richie, but now that it was about to happen, what would I say to him? What would he say to me?

My mom walked with me as far as the reception area, but she stayed there. To get all the way inside, I had to empty my pockets, take off my shoes, go through a metal detector, and then be patted down.

Once I reached the visitors' area, I waited at a small table. When Richie entered, I didn't recognize him. He was wearing an orange jumpsuit and his hair had been cut short, making his ears seem to stick out more than usual. But it was his eyes that tricked me. They were dull and dead, where before they'd always been bright.

The chairs, the tables, the lights, and the carpets—everything about the visiting room was normal, yet I felt as if I were on another planet in another universe, and I could tell Richie felt the same. We couldn't get any conversation going. After a while, he pointed to a table in the corner that had board games on it. "When my dad visits, we play chess," he said. So that's what we ended up doing.

Finally, the half hour was up. A guard came over to the table and nodded to Richie. "See you next week," I said.

Richie stood and headed to the door leading back to his tiny room. After he'd taken a few steps, he turned back. Something almost like a smile crossed his face. "Nobody's going to call you a wuss ever again."

CHAPTER 2

The weeks before Christmas break are hard to describe. In some ways, Crown Hill High returned to normal. I went to the same classes taught by the same teachers to the same students. The McDermotts and my other Whitman friends started talking to me again, though they never mentioned Richie or the shooting. With Anya, it was the opposite. All she wanted to talk about was Richie, but there was nothing new to say.

Hunter and Colton and the rest of those guys—they kept to themselves and they kept quiet. Suicide Alley became just a slightly narrow hallway. And if Hunter saw me anywhere on campus, he dropped his head and stared at his shoes. Mr. Spady avoided me too, and so did Ms. Fontelle, the dance teacher who told me it would all blow over.

One day, Coach Lever called me to his classroom

during his planning period. "I heard you got in to see Richie. How's he doing?"

"Okay, I guess."

He frowned. "They won't let me talk to him on the phone. I went to visit him, but he wouldn't come out to see me."

"He doesn't say much to me when I'm there."

"At least he's talking to somebody." Coach Lever stopped, looked down, and shook his head. "Two things eat at me, Brock. First, that I didn't know my own team. That my players would turn on Richie—I thought we were better than that." He paused. "And the other thing is that Richie shouldn't even have been on the field. You should have been back there. You've got the great hands, and you know the rules. You'd have caught the snap, waited for the double zeros, and then taken a knee. Game over. We win." He paused. "We should be getting ready for a playoff game. Instead—" He stopped and shook his head sadly.

I turned to leave, but his voice stopped me. "You'd tell me, wouldn't you? If you even remotely suspected something like this again. You'd tell me or somebody, right?"

I visited Richie every Saturday. I was nervous each time, but not like I'd been during the first visit. We played chess, and as we played he'd talk about JDC and I'd talk about

Crown Hill High. I tried to tell him what Coach Lever had said, but he wasn't interested.

I couldn't visit Richie on the Saturday before Christmas. My family flew down to San Francisco. A year earlier, I hadn't wanted any of our relatives to see my father. Now, to me, my father didn't even seem sick. His arm braces and his slow movements and his muscle weakness — they were part of who he was.

The visit went okay. We flew back to Seattle on a Friday. Saturday afternoon, I went to see Richie. "Didn't you read the newspaper?" the woman at the first desk said. "He isn't a U.S. citizen, so he's been turned over to the Chinese government. He's in China now, or on his way."

My mother was standing just behind me. She sensed my confusion and stepped forward. "Do you have a phone number for him?"

"No."

"Is there an address?"

"Not that I know of."

"Then how can my son get in touch with Richie?"

The woman shrugged. "I don't think he can."

CHAPTER 3

A numbness came over me then. I was numb walking the halls at Crown Hill, numb in class, and numb doing my homework. When I talked to my mom and dad, I was numb. I said things without knowing what I was saying. I heard things without knowing what I was hearing.

It turns out that you can get along okay when you're numb. If kids told jokes, I laughed; if they were serious, I was serious. I studied enough to get decent grades, and I answered enough questions in class to stay under the radar.

Coach Lever told me he wanted me to play summer-league football in a seven-on-seven league that he was organizing, and then play varsity football for him in the fall. "You need to play again, Brock," he said. "You can't let things end this way."

"I'll think about it," I told him.

He knew I was blowing him off, because after that he

was always pulling me aside in the hallways. He asked me to commit to his league so many times that it became a running joke between us, the only joke I had going those days. "Ready to sign up?" he'd say. "The pen is right here."

"Maybe tomorrow," I'd answer.

In February, Hunter signed a letter of intent to attend college at Humboldt State in California. It didn't bother me, but when Anya heard she was furious. "Richie's probably rotting in some horrible jail in China, and that jerk gets a full scholarship because he can play a stupidly violent game. It's not right."

March meant soccer season. I was going to skip it, but my father insisted I turn out. "You need to do things," he said. "You can't just walk through life."

I didn't want to argue with him, or with anybody. That's part of being numb. And playing goalie for Coach Jacklin was actually better than doing nothing after school. Practices and games made the days go by faster.

Sometimes, though, when the ball was down at the other end of the field and I knew it wasn't coming back for a while, my mind would go back to Richie. Where was he? What was happening to him?

I'd gone online to read about the punishments in China. Wikipedia said minors who committed crimes just had to check in with a neighborhood committee for moral instruction, which didn't sound too bad. But other sites—the ones that Anya must have read—described kids serving years in prison for crimes that seemed really minor.

Richie had come out of nowhere, an Asian kid with big ears who was great at everything. He'd jolted me out of my old life and into a new one. His mom, my dad—we shared things that nobody else could understand. And then he was gone.

Just gone.

How do you accept that?

CHAPTER 4

And then today happened.

We had a soccer game against Lakeside at their field. Their record was 6–0, while we were 2–4. We had no chance to win, and we knew it. On the ride to Lakeside, I looked out the window and saw nothing. Guys around me talked, but I heard nothing. It was just another day to get through.

But once our bus pulled into the Lakeside parking lot and I saw those ivy-covered brick buildings and those perfect green lawns, something ignited inside me. I remembered the last time I'd been there, when Richie had gotten himself kicked out of the game. I'd sucked as a goalkeeper; we'd all sucked; and they'd destroyed us.

I sat up in the seat, fire running through my veins for the first time in a long time. Lakeside wasn't going to destroy us again, not if I could help it. I was going to play the kind of game I should have played a year earlier, the kind of game Richie taught me to play.

Lakeside was better, a lot better, so they dominated the opening minutes, getting chance after chance. But I was unbeatable in goal, stopping every shot that came my way, playing the angles perfectly. Nothing got by me.

My unexpected success gave my teammates a tiny bit of hope. We started winning more fifty-fifty balls; we started getting a few chances of our own. And then we got a kiss from Lady Luck. Just before half, Lakeside's goalie stumbled to one knee on what should have been an easy save. The ball dribbled by him, and before he could recover, Tim McDermott poked it into the net. Lakeside had controlled the game, but we were ahead 1–0.

Still, one goal is nothing against a machine like Lakeside. They'd been scoring four and five goals every game, so there was no panic on their side. But in the second half, I stayed in the zone, making save after save. The time kept ticking away. The Lakeside guys upped the pressure, while their parents and girlfriends screamed for the tying goal. They were the best team in the state. We were nothing. This couldn't be happening. But it was happening. They weren't knocking on the door—they were pounding on it—but I wouldn't let them in. Victory was so close, I could taste it.

And then, in a flash, everything went wrong. Peter

Lee tried to make a long crossing pass, but he caught his foot in the ground, and the ball never got in the air. Instead, it rolled out to the center of the field, where a Lakeside forward took control. He dribbled upfield with uncovered forwards on both sides. Rory challenged, forcing a pass to the right side.

Lakeside's top scorer was coming at me. I took a few steps out to cut his angle. Rory was moving toward him too but was still ten yards off. The Lakeside guy settled the ball, eyed the goal and me, and then drilled a line shot headed toward the lower left corner of the goal. I took two steps and then laid out for the ball, stretching every inch of my body. I felt it hit my fingertips. As I landed on the grass, I looked back toward the net.

The ball bounced once, hit the post, and bounded back onto the field, right in front of the goal. I had no chance to get to it, but Rory hadn't quit on the play. He beat two Lakeside guys to the ball and kicked it over the end line.

Lakeside botched the corner kick. Peter Lee booted the ball the length of the field, and seconds later the referee blew his whistle. We'd done it. We'd beaten Lakeside 1–0 on their field. We shook their hands and said good game, wearing our game faces, but back on the bus we hollered like maniacs.

When I got home, I went upstairs and opened my laptop. Fireworks were going off in my brain. It felt great to feel alive again. I had to tell someone. I had to keep the numbness away.

But who? Who?

When the answer came, my excitement vanished in the same way that fireworks disappear into the night sky.

It was Richie I wanted to tell. No one else.

I sat back in my chair and stared at my computer. I didn't even have enough energy to close it down—I just sat and watched the cursor blink at me.

I don't know how long I'd been staring at the screen when a message popped up in the right-hand corner of the screen. I didn't read it, but it half registered before disappearing. The cursor blinked a few more times, and then I sat straight up.

Had I seen what I thought I'd seen?

I went to my bookmarks and opened Red Hot Pawn. In bold letters, a message flashed across the screen: *Vampire17 has challenged you to a game. Do you accept?*

My hands were shaking as I clicked *Yes*, and a chessboard filled the screen. Richie had made his first move: Pawn to King Four. In the message box, he'd written, *Doing okay. How about you?*

I leaned back in my chair, took a couple of deep breaths, and made my move. King's Knight to Bishop Three. Then I clicked on the message box. I had five hundred characters. I typed a question, then deleted it. I typed another and deleted that. I had so much I wanted to know—where should I start? I looked up the ceiling, and suddenly I realized what I wrote didn't matter. There'd be time.

There'd be plenty of time.

I quickly typed, *Beat Lakeside today. You should have seen their faces.*

We played for the next twenty minutes, exchanging short messages with each move, easing our way back.

Rematch tomorrow? I typed when checkmate was a move away.

Day after he replied with his winning move. *School placement test tomorrow. My Chinese still sucks, but it's getting better. Back at it.*

My parents came home a few minutes after I'd logged off. I told them about Richie, and then about beating Lakeside. I must have talked a lot, and fast, because my mom said she was excited to see me excited. "You need to get back into things."

My dad nodded.

I ate a microwaved pizza and then went upstairs to my room, where I played video games and watched a Warriors-Lakers game on ESPN. I took a shower and tried to sleep but couldn't. Just after one a.m., I realized I hadn't told Anya. It was too late to call, so I texted her: *Call me as soon as you read this.*

I was about to turn off the light to try again to get some real sleep, but something still was wrong. One more thing needed doing, but as I lay there—my mind working—I couldn't figure out what it was.

And then I knew.

I opened my laptop, went to the school website, and found a link to Coach Lever's email.

If there's still room on that seven-on-seven team, you can put my name down. I'll be playing next year. Brock Ripley.

CARL DEUKER is a premier author of provocative psychological sports fiction. A teacher for many years in the Northshore school district, he lives in Seattle, Washington, with his family.